INTO
THE
DARKNESS

Book Two of THE FOUNDATIONS OF HOPE Trilogy

LEATHEL GRODY

Lethal Publishing Corporation

INTO THE DARKNESS

Book Two of THE FOUNDATIONS OF HOPE Trilogy
www.foundationsofhope.com

A Lethal, Inc Book
Published by the Lethal Publishing Corporation
P.O. Box 1057
Kalkaska, Mi 49646
Visit our website at www.lethalpublishing.com

Cover and interior art by Leathel Grody

Edited by:
JoEtta Dingman
Rick Rindt

ISBN-10: 1-59787-004-8
ISBN-13: 978-1-59787-004-7

Printed in the United States of America
10 9 8 7 6 5 4 3 2 1

ACKNOWLEDGMENTS

I once again would like to thank my wife for her understanding during all my Foundations projects(books and game).

I also would like to thank the editors, JoEtta Dingman and Rick Rindt, again. Thanks for putting up with my last minute writing habits.

A special thank you to the proof readers of ItD:
Tracey J. Pickard
Davida and the rest of the Greene family
Clay Skrzypczak
Andy Blodgett

I have appreciated your comments. suggestions, and enthusiasm.

Shield and Sword Forms

Level 1) Defense of the Tortoise (Defensive)
Level 2) Attack of the Armadillo
Level 3) Towering Oak
Level 4) Stance of the Boulder
Level 5) Hibernating Bear

Level 6) Baaing of the Lamb (Defensive)
Level 7) Fog in the Morning
Level 8) Bite of the Wolf
Level 9) Charging Stag
Level 10) Swarm of the Locusts

Level 11) Wind in the Mountains (Defensive)
Level 12) Laugh of the Hyena
Level 13) Stampede of the Buffalo
Level 14) Prowling Tiger
Level 15) Strike of the Cobra

Level 16) Cornered Badger (Defensive)
Level 17) Attack of the Mongoose
Level 18) Chase of the Mustang
Level 19) Dance of the Sea
Level 20) Attack of the Lion

Level 21) Fortress (Defensive)
Level 22) Stings of the Swarm
Level 23) Strike of the Eagle
Level 24) Charging Rhino
Level 25) Eye of the Storm

Level 26) *********(Defensive)
Level 27) Dance of Death
Level 28) *********
Level 29) *********
Level 30) *********

Lansing

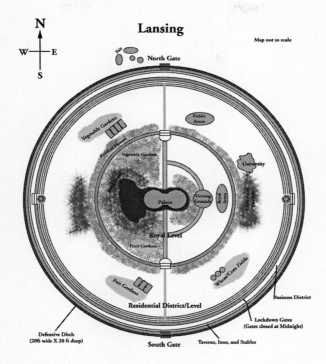

Map not to scale

N
W — E
S

North Gate

Vegetable Gardens

Public Arena

Festival District

Vegetable Gardens

University

Palace

Viewing Grounds

Royal Arena

Royal Level

Fruit Gardens

Fruit Gardens

Wheat/Corn Fields

Residential District/Level

Business District

Lockdown Gates
(Gates closed at Midnight)

Defensive Ditch
(20ft wide X 20 ft deep)

South Gate

Taverns, Inns, and Stables

r=2 mile
d=2r=4 miles
C=12.56 miles
K=Area=12.56 miles sq

Table of Contents

INTO
THE
DARKNESS

Book Two of THE FOUNDATIONS OF HOPE Trilogy

LEATHEL GRODY

CHAPTER ONE
All According to Plan

"In preparing for battle I have always found that plans are useless, but planning is indispensable."

— Dwight D. Eisenhower (1890 - 1969)

"I believe that unarmed truth and unconditional love will have the final word in reality. This is why right, temporarily defeated, is stronger than evil triumphant." — Martin Luther King Jr. (1929 - 1968)

EKRA LOOKED over the battlefield and smiled. Hundreds of Saurians and thousands of humans lay dead around the walled city the humans called Lansing. The humans had protected Lansing, but in doing so, they had destroyed the rest of the country.

For many human years she had plotted every last detail of her campaign, and finally those plans were beginning to take shape. The human and Saurian death toll from this small battle was a minute achievement, and she relished the fact that this battle was only a glimpse of what was yet to come. She could not wait until the humans were eradicated. The Saurian species would be eliminated as well. The Earth would be left to her and her kind.

Ekra sniffed the air. She could only smell one from the human lineage she had come to abhore. She hoped the child was dead. That left only one of the lineage to be destroyed. He was within the city, but that did not matter. She would wait for another day. His usefulness had reached its limit and it was time to finish the task she had started decades ago. The human man's hidden protector would not succeed in protecting him. Ekra did not know who or what it was that protected the man, but she had already calculated accordingly. Ekra would leverage all the protection the hidden one would use into her own plans.

It was time. The foolish Saurian queen needed to finish her part and be guided accordingly.

CHAPTER TWO
Prince Daniel Lancaster

"There is only one difference between a madman and me. I am not mad."
- Salvador Dali (1904 - 1989)

D ANIEL HIT the bed with his fist. "I'll kill them all if I have to, Markos," Daniel said, flinching in pain from his sudden movement.

Markos raised a questioning eyebrow at the comment.

Daniel laid his head back down on the pillow and sighed. He knew exactly what Markos meant. He was not the same person he once was, and he now followed a different path.

"Your Highness, the word has spread among my men. If the council has tried to hide Rebekah underground, my men will know," a deep grating voice said from behind the King's Guards standing around his bed.

A path cleared between two guards and the largest man Daniel had ever seen stood between them. The King's Guards were extraordinarily tall men, but this black-skinned man made even the guards look up at him. His height only added to his width. The man was easily a chest and a half wider than Daniel, and his arms were twice the size of Daniel's own. Daniel had heard of The General of the Outlaw City and the rumors about his size, but to look up at the seven foot tall man while lying down in a bed was an unnerving experience.

"General, it is an honor to meet you. Some say you worked and fought side-by-side with Rebekah. A friend of Rebekah's is a friend of mine."

The giant bowed to Daniel. "Your Highness, it is an honor to meet the one who trained the Princess. She is a remarkable person."

The lead guard stepped forward. "Prince Daniel, we will find her. Each one of us takes her kidnapping as a personal failure and we dedicate our spare time to gain back our honor." The King's Guard finished, then raised his fist to his chest in salute. The eight other guards standing on duty around the bed brought a fist their chest in agreement. Daniel nodded and slowly brought his fist to his own chest.

"I hope it will not come to that, Squad Leader Joshua."

Daniel looked around the palace room, watching the other guards drop their salutes. He had recently awaken from his three day sleep to find out his daughter, Rebekah, had been taken. From the recent battle he still could envision the tall Guard's red plumes a hundred feet away. He had searched so long to find his daughter, only to get so close and get an arrow shot into his chest. Most of these guards with their tall red plumes on the top of their helms were the ones Daniel had seen during the battle. Rebekah had been in the middle of them, leading the citizens of Lansing out of the city to break the lizard creatures' siege.

"Nor I, Your Highness. We may soon find the captors turning themselves in once they find out the hornet's nest they have captured. In the short time I have known her, I've learned that the Princess can take care of herself, and she will make her captors pay for what they have done," Joshua said.

Daniel could not help but laugh. The laughing hurt, but it also felt good. He knew Joshua was not joking in the least. "I do not laugh at your comment. I raised Rebekah for fifteen years, and I agree wholeheartedly." Daniel's face grew serious. "You said you had news about the King's Council, Joshua?"

"Yes, Your Highness. The council is currently in a meeting, again scheming new plans." Joshua paused, then continued, "I mean again, as in they tried to meet in private once after the Princess took control of the country. She… well," Joshua smiled, "she eradicated such ideas and repositioned their egos."

Daniel was taken aback by the slight smirks that formed on the King's Guards faces. The King's Guard rarely smiled while on duty. He'd have to find out about the matter.

Markos stepped closer. "We only let the matter come to you because of its seriousness. Daniel, you need to take control of the country."

Daniel laid his head back on the pillow and sighed. He had never wanted the position or power of his birthright. A quiet life, living with his wife and daughter, had been his dream. That dream had been shattered sixteen years ago when his wife had mysteriously died during Rebekah's birth. With Rebekah missing and his brother dethroned, he knew he had no choice.

"I will take rule of Rembelshem until Rebekah gets back. From then I will act as her advisor," Daniel said.

Daniel pushed himself to a sitting position and cringed at the pain in his left side and chest. During the breaking of the siege of Lansing, Daniel had been shot with an arrow in the chest and stabbed with a sword in his left side. Daniel lifted his overnight shirt to look at his wounds, or at least where his wounds should have been.

"I know it wasn't a dream," Daniel said in confusion.

Markos laid a hand on Daniel's shoulder. "It was taken care of."

Daniel nodded. Markos was a Paladin, a warrior of God. Paladins were given gifts, or special powers, to help them fight the unusual evil battles they faced. There were battles for humans to fight, and then there were the battles no normal human could fight.

Daniel kicked his feet over the side of his bed. The pain in his side was excruciating. Though his wounds were no longer visible, the pain was still there. He felt lightheaded, and darkness began to encompass his vision. Daniel closed his eyes and took a deep breath, taking control before he passed out.

"Your Highness, it may not be wise for you to get out of bed. We can put the council under house arrest until you have had more rest," Joshua said.

Daniel's vision cleared and he stood from the bed. "Thank you, Squad Leader Joshua, but I will be fine. You would actually be willing to upset the Council and put them under house arrest?"

Daniel was astonished to see each of the guards smirk again. "Rebekah didn't?" Daniel asked in amusement.

"You might say the King's Guards are currently not on any of the council's most favorite list," Joshua answered.

Daniel smiled and shook his head. Rebekah must have given the Council quite an awakening.

"Markos, if you'll excuse me, I need to prepare."

Markos bowed and exited the room. The King's Guard followed and repositioned themselves outside Daniel's door.

Daniel quickly washed and found clothes that had been brought to his room. It was strange to wear the overtly ornamental clothing again. Since the night he snuck out of Lansing with his newborn daughter, Daniel had worn clothing that a common citizen of Rembelshem would wear.

Daniel rubbed his chin as he thought. The scratchiness of his beard took him by surprise. He had never had a beard while living in the Royal Palace. Daniel looked in the mirror and brushed his chin. He had begun growing the beard the night he vanished as Prince Daniel Lancaster. The council would react more favorably if he looked like Prince Daniel. Daniel found the razor and removed sixteen years of hiding. With his brother removed from power, he no longer needed to fear for his or his daughter's safety.

Once finished, Daniel peered in the mirror again. It was strange to look at the resemblance of the man he once was. He looked and felt older than that other man. That was another life or more like another-life time ago.

Daniel looked in a six-foot high mirror. There was one thing missing to complete the presence he needed to portray. Daniel searched and found his Weapons Master sword leaning against the wall next to his bed. Daniel smiled. He would guess Markos had something to do with making sure it was nearby. Once his enemy and now his friend, Markos and he were much alike.

Daniel opened the door and the guards stood at attention. Markos stood nearby talking with a blonde, thirty-something man Daniel did not know. But from his stance and awareness, Daniel knew what he was. Daniel laid his left hand on the hilt of his sword. The position was not as apparent nor as effective as using his right hand across his body to prepare to draw his sword if needed, but stealth in some situations was better. Only one trained to a high level would know that he was not just resting his hand, but that he was prepared to deliver a reverse strike or defense technique if needed. Markos fortunately was one of those men.

"Daniel, I would like to introduce Special Forces member Jordan Sinclair," Markos said, motioning to the blonde haired man. "He notified Rebekah of the Council's first meeting and he was the one to bring it to our attention this time as well."

Jordan stepped forward and bowed. "Prince Daniel, it is an honor to meet you. You are still a legend among the Special Forces teams."

The man wore no sword, but that would not stop a Special Forces member from killing his target if that was the objective. Daniel continued to hold a firm grip on his sword.

"That was a different man and another lifetime ago, but my appreciation is given for helping my daughter."

Jordan backed away and kept an eye on Daniel's sword. "At least another lifetime ago."

Daniel smiled. This one was a higher ranking member of the Special Forces team. "Jordan, how is that one in your position would be in the castle so often and know of its happenings?"

"King Robert assigned me to watch over the castle and provide security in a different manner than the King's Guards provide. They have their abilities, and as you know, we have been trained to have our own."

Daniel nodded. The King's Guards were menacing figures in appearance and talent. Each guard stood a minimum of six and a half feet tall and their large red feathered helms provided another foot to their foreboding appearance. Daniel and Markos were taller than average men, but surrounded by the guards, they did not appear to be so. Daniel looked at Jordan.

While the guards were the visible security, Jordan, and probably others, provided a stealth security throughout the hallways of the castle.

Daniel motioned with his hand. "Somebody please lead. We have the Council of Greed to deal with again."

The guards positioned themselves in a formation around Daniel and waited for Daniel's command. "Continue," Daniel said to start the guards walking.

Daniel watched his surroundings as he walked through the hallways and finally down the large circular stairs down into the Royal Palace's entryway. It had been sixteen years since he had been in the castle. Mixed feelings rushed through him. For most of his life this palace had been his home. There were many good and bad memories during those years. But the second part of his life he had lived as an innkeeper in his inn with only his daughter. Daniel smiled. It had been a small wooden inn, nothing to compare to the luxuries of the palace, but it held all good memories. None he would ever want to trade for the riches of the castle.

Palace workers stared as he and the guards

marched down the east stairs, through the open large grand entrance way, and up the stairs leading to the western half of the Royal Palace. He was sure they all had heard the rumors that he was actually still alive. It must have been a sight for them to finally see Prince Daniel walking through the hallways after so many years.

Down the hallway Daniel saw Council Guards standing outside a doorway. As they saw the large formation of the King's Guard approach, the Council Guards removed their swords, and one started to reach for the door. Abruptly, the two guards silently fell to the ground before they could alert the council members. Jordan walked from the opposite end of the hallway and retrieved tranquilizer blow darts from his victims. Daniel knew he had guessed correctly about Jordan's abilities.

Jordan looked at Daniel. "The council will have more guards with them in the room this time. They were not pleased by their last surprise visit."

Daniel looked at the King's Guards. "Deal with the council guards. I'll deal with the council."

Markos laid a hand on Daniel's shoulder.

"Daniel, you are not that man anymore."

Daniel laid his hand on Markos's shoulder and locked arms with him. "Fear not my friend. The council does not know that," Daniel said with a smile. "Markos, you must know I never wanted any of this. A simple life with Hannah and Rebekah was all I hoped for."

"I know that now. My sister would have been pleased to live such a life with you."

Daniel nodded to Squad Leader Joshua, then the nine guards burst into the room. Yelling and shouting erupted from the room, followed by the sounds of armor against armor. The yelling and verbal assaults on the King's Guard grew louder. Daniel removed his sword and entered the room, dragging his sword on the marble floor. The yelling in the room quickly ceased as everyone looked toward the high-pitched screeching noise.

Daniel swayed his head and body as if listening to some unknown music. He let his sword drag on the ground, swaying with the movement of his body. He knew, or at least hoped, he looked like he had lost his mind. He must be playing the part well.

All eyes, even the King's Guards, were focused on his Weapons Master sword. A Special Forces officer combined with a Weapons Master who had lost his wits was not a desirable combination.

Daniel quickly swung his sword between two of the closest council members and lodged it deeply into the large wooden table. The two council members jumped back in their seats, but Daniel did not focus his attention on them. He squinted, and tilted his head, looking at his sword, as if pondering how it had gotten there.

As if waking from a trance, Daniel spoke. "Council Members. How good it is to see you once again." Daniel looked around the room. He recognized most of the faces. The faces were more plump and older than the last time he had seen them, but they still held the same greed in their eyes. "It has been brought to my attention that one or more of you had an involvement in the disappearance of the Princess." Daniel made eye contact with each of the council members. Whether old or new, they all knew who he was and what he was capable of. Behind the council stood the King's Guards, holding the Council Guards on the floor with a foot or spear butt. The light from the hallway diminished. He did not need to look to know Markos was standing in the doorway. With Markos standing in the door, and the General outside the room, no one would leave the room without Daniel's permission.

A younger member tried to speak, but Daniel raised his hand. "Now Council Members, the fact that one of you is responsible for my daughter's disappearance upsets me greatly. Each of you will be interrogated in a manner I see fit. You are no longer under the protection of my brother and I will do to you what must be done to get the answers I need."

"Squad Leader, please escort the council and their guards to their rooms. Their interrogation will begin when I am ready. If any of them dare to resist, well, just ensure they stay alive long enough for me to get the information I need from them."

Daniel removed his sword from the table and stepped toward Markos, who had entered the room to clear the doorway. Daniel watched as the council members and their guards were escorted out of the room by the King's Guard. Daniel followed the guards, Markos, and Jordan as the General trailed from behind.

At the bottom of the stairs a new set of King's Guards took formation around Daniel as the previous guards escorted their charges to their rooms.

"Markos, will you meet with me in an hour? We must discuss our plans to find Rebekah. Jordan, thank you for your dedication to the Lancaster family."

On command, the guards led Daniel to his room. He entered and closed the door. Finally alone in his room, Daniel rubbed his side. He had gritted his teeth through the whole ordeal, but the pain had always been there. He had used the pain to fuel his anger with the meeting with the council. But now alone he just wanted to rest. Removing his belt and sword helped ease the pressure. He tossed the sword on his bed and sat at his desk to look at maps of the known countries. Rebekah was out there somewhere and he would find her no matter what.

The wind blew, and the drapes of the window rustled. Daniel looked to the window and his heart jumped. A Saurian woman in a long white dress stood in his room next to his window.

CHAPTER THREE
Human Slave Camp

"In the middle of every difficulty lies opportunity." - Albert Einstein (1879 - 1955)

"For even hereunto were ye called: because Christ also suffered for us, leaving us an example, that ye should follow his steps." - I Peter 2:21

R EBEKAH'S HEAD POUNDED. She kept her eyes closed, listening to her surroundings. From the sounds and feeling, she guessed she was in the back of a horse drawn wagon. The bumps in the road were lifting her body and then slamming her head onto the bottom of the wooden cart.

The last thing Rebekah could remember was meeting with a man in the Royal Palace who tricked her with Saurians that could turn invisible. She was not sure how that was even possible. She was supposed to be protected from the Saurian mind tricks by the belief in her God.

Rebekah slowly opened her eyes. She already could tell it was midday by the brightness seeping through her closed eyelids and the warmth of the sun upon her skin. Rebekah thought she would be prepared for any sight, but she hadn't been. She would never have guessed her uncle, King Robert, would be seated next to her and staring down at her.

"Good afternoon, Princess," the King said solemnly.

He sat against the back railing, swaying with the motion of the cart. Rebekah was not sure how to respond. It was rather awkward considering her situation. She looked around and saw Saurian soldiers walking beside and behind the cart. Strangely enough, the humanoid lizard creatures did not bother Rebekah as much as the man sitting next to her did. She could not help but look at the stump of his right arm.

"Where are we?" Rebekah finally decided to respond.

"Heading east into The Republic, now that the borders are no longer protected."

"I was not the one who called the army away from its position from the borders if that is what you are insinuating," Rebekah said, pushing herself into a sitting position against the side railing of the wagon.

Rebekah glanced at the lizard creature walking a few feet away from where she sat. It wore the more common red leather armor Rebekah was used to seeing. The creature walked like a human, and was able to trick most humans into seeing an illusion that it was a human, but Rebekah could see the lizard head sticking out of the breastplate armor.

"Then who did? Only you would have had the power to…" the King paused. "It was your father,

Daniel? I knew he was the one leading the people of Lansing against me."

Rebekah shook her head. "The person leading the people was The General of Troit. I have not seen my father for six months."

"The General has finally turned against me," King Robert spoke louder. "I will have him strapped when I am out of this mess."

"You forget. You have no power to do such a thing. I have relieved you of your duty," Rebekah said harshly.

Robert rubbed the stub of his right arm. The arm had been cleanly severed a few inches below the elbow. "It is quite hard not to forget, Princess. But remember, your own governing powers have been seized from you as well," Robert said. "Yours, or your father's actions have cost the rest of the humans their freedom and their lives."

Rebekah cringed at the sight of the previous King's arm. It was not the arm itself that bothered Rebekah, but how the arm had come to be in its current state. She had been the one to sever the it. She still did not know what had exactly happened, just the sword of fire that had appeared in her hands at a desperate time. Rebekah shuddered.

The King's statement bothered Rebekah. It reminded her of the King's Council member that had tricked her into being caught. He had said the Saurians had used all the good she had achieved and used it to benefit them. She had been a pawn used by the enemy and she didn't like it. She finally grasped what was bothering her. The General's grandma had said something that she had never paid attention to and, as Grandma had said, she would understand later. She had said, "all the good you do in the world might end up looking bad, but all the bad will end up being for the good."

Rebekah smiled and looked at her surroundings. Seated next to her was a man who would gladly kill her and walking all around her were the Saurians, which would not give a second thought to killing her. Her father's brother was startled by the strange smile. She did not know how, but her current situation was for a purpose. A few months earlier, on her way to the Outlaw City, she had thought that 'She may only be a pawn in this giant game, but she would play her part well. She would be the hands and feet of God and walk steadfast into a city of vipers if it was required of her.' Rebekah chuckled as she looked at the snake-like head of the Saurian guard walking next to her. This time she literally was going to be with vipers.

* * * *

REBEKAH GUESSED the trip to their destination had taken a couple of weeks. From the heat and humidity, her Uncle had guessed they were in the southern coastline areas of The Republic. Rebekah and Robert had concluded that they were following the Saurian army as it demolished the cities in its path. Rebekah watched as her uncle Robert's attitude grew darker with each village. Unbeknownst to Rebekah, until her final minutes before being taken as a captive, her grandfather and her uncle, the previous kings of Rembelshem, had built the largest army in the lands in order to protect their country from the Saurian threat. What had been perceived as paranoid leaders worried about neighboring countries' attacks had actually been cautious leaders striving to protect the

Rembelshem citizens against the lizard creatures. Now all that the former king had worked to protect had been destroyed in less than a week.

A horn blowing at the front of the caravan startled Rebekah. She tried to peer over the wall of the wagon but could not see what was happening.

"I believe we have arrived at our destination," Robert said. He was a head taller than she was and did not have the obstacles blocking his line of site. He squinted, sighed, and shook his head. "It looks to possibly be some kind of slave camp. I can see wooden pens with humans in them. I didn't think these creatures took slaves."

"What I have learned is that the Saurians are *cleansing* the earth of the humans, as they put it, and taking the countries' leaders as slaves. I am guessing that they gather the more educated to have the best slaves possible."

"These creatures are not as intelligent as they say if they think the leaders of countries are the smartest of the human stock. Most leaders are in position by greed, trickery, or birth."

The sarcastic tone of her uncle surprised

Rebekah. As a king he himself was known to have all of those traits and more. She had recently discovered that her father was not the man she had believed he was, and now she was finding out that her uncle seemed to be far different than most perceived him to be.

The wagon stopped abruptly and Rebekah banged the back of her head on the wagon's front wall. The heat had already been causing her a mild headache, but now the throbbing in her temples was nauseating.

A Saurian guard opened the back of the wagon and another prodded them with a spear as he directed them off. Rebekah and her uncle were led into a cell with eight other humans and… Rebekah had to take a second glance. A Saurian female was also in the cell among the other humans. Rebekah could only guess the Saurian female was mentally disguising herself as a human. None of the captives knew of the spy among them.

Besides the female lizard creature, there were a wide variety of humans in the cell. A young girl of about twelve looked to be the youngest, with a balding, plump, elderly man as the oldest. Rebekah counted ten in all, including the Saurian.

The young girl broke away from the huddled group and clasped Rebekah's hand. She nervously glanced at the Saurian guards pushing Rebekah and Robert into the cell.

"Come. Come," the girl said, pulling Rebekah's hand.

Rebekah let herself be pulled to the back of the cell wall. The little girl wore a tattered, yellow sun dress and continued to speak quickly in the Dangarian language. Rebekah only knew a few words and could not understand what the little girl was trying to say. Instead of concentrating on what she could not do, Rebekah focused her attention on her surroundings. Items in the cell to use as weapons were minimal. The ground held a few twigs and rocks with small clumps of grass that had survived under the footsteps of the prisoners.

Three older teenage boys approached Rebekah and her uncle. The one leading the group spoke harshly in the Dangarian language to the young girl and reached for her. Rebekah instinctively responded by grabbing his wrist and twisting. His elbow torqued inward and upward in an awkward position causing him to drop to his knees. If it were life and death, Rebekah could easily have applied more pressure and dislocated his shoulder. She hoped it would not come to that. She let go of the boy's wrist and pushed him back.

The boy had been taken off guard. He rubbed his wrist and pumped up his chest. His two companions stepped beside him.

"How dare you touch me, servant. I am Prince Alberto DeLango. Eldest prince of Dangaria. You shall be punished for your insolence. My sister was happy to have another girl here, but she should not be touching someone such as you."

Rebekah wanted to laugh. She and her uncle were covered in dust and sweat and must have looked a horrible mess. Yet, little did the prince know that the man beside her was, or at least used to be, King Robert Lancaster. One of the most feared leaders of the three countries. The armies he controlled were larger than both the other two countries combined. On the other hand, she might be the Princess Rebekah of Rembelshem, but she had been raised as an innkeeper's daughter all her life. She was used to dealing with patrons from her father's inn whose heads were bloated with pride. Her faith would not allow her take pride in her new position, nor did her father raise her care about such things.

Her uncle on the other hand, was not as reserved, and stepped forward. He grabbed the teen around the neck.

"Listen here you little filth. I am King Robert Lancaster of Rembelshem. I command armies large enough to squash your country just as I could crush your neck right now."

Robert pushed the boy back into his two friends.He waited for an attack back, but none came. Even the Prince knew who Robert was. Rebekah wondered what the other countries really said about her uncle. His own country feared him.

"Thank you," Rebekah said.

"You are highly mistaken if you think I did that for you. You are on your own, Princess. Good luck," King Robert said and turned away from her.

CHAPTER FOUR
Human Sympathizer

"The pessimist sees difficulty in every opportunity. The optimist sees the opportunity in every difficulty." - Sir Winston Churchill (1874 - 1965)

D ANIEL INSTINCTIVELY REACHED for his sword on his belt, but it was not there. He glanced over and saw it lying on the bed. It was too far away. He eyed the desk and saw twenty different objects he could turn into weapons instead.

"Who are you?" Daniel asked, standing and leaning on his desk. His fingers gently rolled a pencil into his palm.

"Your Majesty, I am Council Member Gilmartin's wife. I come with information about your daughter."

"First of all, it is Your Highness, as I am only a prince, not the King. Secondly, you are a Saurian, so do not play your guise with me. You have five seconds before you die."

Daniel found it interesting to watch the Saurian's face show shock from his statement. She was only ten feet away. No armor, no weapons; he would give her ten seconds before she met the tip of his pencil.

The lizard creature composed herself quickly and continued, "So it is true. There are humans that have evolved enough to block our simple mind illusion. Fascinating."

"State your purpose, creature," Daniel said harshly.

The creature put a wrist to her nose. "My purpose, *human*, is that I do come with information about your offspring. Although I am not terribly fond of your awful smelling kind, I belong to a group that does not agree with the genocide of your species. Your daughter and brother are being taken to the southern peninsula of your lands. The Queen has requested the rulers of the upper lands be taken there for training as slaves. Our Glorious Queen feels that your rulers are some of the few worthy to keep alive after we cleanse your lands."

"Can you be more specific as to the location of my daughter?"

"It is true you upper land humans are not very smart. Listen human. She is in the southern peninsula of your lands. More specifically, the lands of The Republic. The sun's position in that location is far more pleasing to my kind than the colder weather of the north. If I receive more information, I will contact you."

Daniel was at a loss. His body was wound tight, ready to launch himself at the creature. On the other hand, if she could find more information he would have to let her go. He felt every Saurian should die. From the Saurian's comments, there were divisions even in their own race. *Divide and conquer*. He would have to let this Saurian go.

The Saurian walked closer to the window, paused, and turned to Daniel. "Watch yourself, *Your Highness*. Your position marks you as it did your offspring." She then jumped out the five story window.

* * * *

"WHAT DO you think, Markos?"

"From my dealings with the Saurians, I am not sure they lie too often. I cannot think of any other reason for her to disclose the information, except the truth."

Daniel nodded. A map of The Republic was spread across his desk. Daniel sat in his chair while Markos, Jordan, Joshua, and the General stood around his desk.

Squad Leader Joshua walked over to the window and leaned out. "Markos, did the Saurian you spoke with say they could fly as well?"

"No. That bothers me. There are many things we do not know about the Saurians, though," Markos replied.

"Jordan, I would like you to build a Special Forces team, probably about eight men, to scout this location and if possible, bring the Princess back."

Jordan bowed. "Yes, Your Highness. I will prepare and ready a team immediately."

"Your Highness, I have my own duties to attend to and I will scout this region as well," Markos said.

"No, I need you here," Daniel stated bluntly.

Markos raised an eyebrow at the statement.

Daniel bit his lip. "I am sorry, Markos. A Paladin is not governed by any ruler, but as my friend, I only wish you to stay."

"You can trust the council of Phillip, the General, and the guards. My skills are pretty useless in ruling a country." Markos smiled. "I am particularly more useful in scouting life-threatening terrain, though."

"Me, too," Daniel replied with a smile. Daniel thought for a second and looked at Jordan. "Jordan, it is rumored somebody called Jarod the Great single-handedly killed thirty of the creatures during the battle against the siege. You may want to find out who he is."

"Yes, Your Highness. He is already on my list."

CHAPTER FIVE
The Special Forces

"The best thing about the future is that it only comes one day at a time."
- Abraham Lincoln (1809 - 1865)

"Be not afraid of greatness: some men are born great, some achieve greatness and some have greatness thrust upon them."

- William Shakespeare (1564 - 1616), 'Twelfth Night'

A CHILD'S LAUGHTER split the silence of the army encampment.

"Do it again Jarod, do it again," the shrill little voice yelled in delight.

The blonde, curly-haired, five-year-old rode on the back of a muscular teenage boy. Jarod laughed and breathed heavily, resting on his hands and knees. "All done, Thad. You've been given a ride around the whole camp," Jarod paused, "twice."

Thadius slid off Jarod's back. "Tomorrow?" Thadius asked.

Jarod laughed. He stood and stretched his throbbing arms as he looked at the surroundings. The army encampment stretched in either direction as far as he could see. Cooking pots hung over open fires as the men of the army began to wake and prepare their breakfasts. Jarod and Thadius had met and made many friends during their journey around the army. Both were well-known. Thadius was considered the catalyst that broke the siege, and stories of Jarod's achievements on the battlefield had spread quickly. Jarod the Great was said to have slain thirty to fifty Saurians by himself. He hated that name and he disliked the rumors spreading of things he had not done, or at least of events he was not sure he had done. Everything had happened so fast during the battle that it was all blurred together. He could still hear Thadius's screams as the swarms of lizard creatures attacked from all around both of them. He was not sure how many he had killed before the army had finally arrived, nor did he care. Thadius was alive and that was what mattered most to him.

Jarod looked at Thadius. "Yes, maybe tomorrow. I hope the city has settled down enough that we can go back in and see if we can find Paladin Markos. I am sure he is worried about you."

"Can we go find Uncle Markos now, Jarod?"

"Not until after breakfast. I am sure Cook Ordell has a plate full of pancakes for you."

Thadius grinned and quickly ran off toward the cook's wagon.

Jarod smiled and walked after the boy. Jarod would miss Thadius. With all that had happened, the boy still looked at life with such innocence. Jarod sighed. It would be for the best. He was only sixteen himself. Daniel Smith the Innkeeper had left a note that Jarod was safe and traveling to Lansing, but Jarod's family, if alive, would still be worried. Jarod smiled. His family would not recognize him. His long hair was now cut short, and he was not the thin, skinny Jarod they once knew.

Jarod walked around the end of Cook Ordell's wagon and snapped out of his daydreaming. Thadius was busily eating a plate of pancakes, but the cook was talking to another man. Jarod did not know who he was, but his outfit indicated what he was. Jarod had crossed paths with a Special Forces team and it had almost not ended well, and now there was another. Jarod's sword rested against the front of the wagon behind the man. It did not matter. Jarod had learned to never rely on any specific weapon. He had already spotted at least ten nearby items that he could use if necessary.

The cook noticed Jarod and raised a hand in acknowledgement. "Ah, Jarod, there you are. I'd like to introduce you to Senior Special Forces Officer Jordan. Prince Daniel himself has sent Jordan to find you."

The situation was not exactly what Jarod was

expecting. His new name of Jarod the Great also had rumors associated with it that he was a Paladin or a Weapons Master. Jarod feared more men would need to try and prove that he was neither. Men had already tried and failed. Jarod did not know what he was, but he knew who had given him his special abilities.

Jarod was used to the strange face many made whenever they first found out he was Jarod the Great. Most expected an older, seasoned warrior, not a young teenage boy.

Jordan paused and turned back to the cook. "I, I am sorry, there must be a mistake. I am looking for Jarod the Great."

The plump cook laughed knowingly and slapped a hand on Jordan's back. "I assure you, Sir, this is Jarod the Great. Give him two swords and you and a team of Special Forces members will still lose."

"Cook Ordell, please," Jarod pleaded. The cook knew Jarod hated the boasting about his talents.

"Special Forces Officer Jordan, please disregard Sir Ordell's challenge. I really do not wish to challenge anybody."

"You do not deny the name of Jarod the Great,

though?"

"No, sir. Although I do not like the name, I cannot deny it."

Without looking, Jordan reached behind himself and picked up Jarod's sword. Jordan tossed the sheathed sword to Jarod. Jarod smiled. He knew if he had been forced to fight, going for the sword would have been a mistake. Jordan would have been waiting for it.

"I'll warn you, son. My duties are my life. I have been assigned to create a team for an important mission and you have been requested personally by Prince Daniel. Otherwise, I would have walked away by now. I will not be gentle with you. If you have been misguiding others, they will find out now."

Jarod sighed. He knew the name was going to come back to haunt him sometime in the future. But on the other hand, he had been specifically requested by the Prince for some type of mission. Six months ago, he was Jarod the Loser at school, and now a prince knew about him. Jarod was not sure what to think or make of it.

Jordan's expression changed to confusion and

his eyes focused behind Jarod. The sound of swords being drawn alerted Jarod to what was going on.

"Is there a problem here, Jarod?" a man asked from behind Jarod.

"No problems, Captain Darian. Special Officer Jordan has requested a *lesson*," Jarod said.

"Ha! Finally, a lesson of yours that doesn't involve one of my troops. Everybody stand down. This should be interesting."

Jordan looked at Cook Ordell. "Watch Thadius, please?"

The cook nodded.

Jordan did not wait for the normal sparring standard of bowing, but launched an overhead strike at Jarod. *Wind in the Mountains.* The defensive sword technique flashed through Jarod's mind. Jarod parried Jordan's attack with his sheathed sword. For the brief second of contact, Jarod used his scabbard to control Jordan's sword defensively and used his left hand to draw his sword from the upside down scabbard and slashed at Jordan's foot.

Jordan lifted his foot and blocked Jarod's swing with the bottom of his foot. Metal clanged against metal. Jarod was caught off guard slightly by somebody wearing metallic boots, but he quickly refocused. Jordan broke past Jarod's scabbard guard and slashed at Jarod. Jarod was forced to roll to the ground underneath the sword but brought his scabbard hard up against Jordan's ribs.

Jarod barely heard the groans from the crowd as the world disappeared. He was forced to focus entirely on Jordan, who was attacking with quick, multiple tactics. Jarod had to agree. Jordan was the best challenger he had ever had.

Jarod kept the defensive, letting Jordan continue the attacks. The Special Forces Officer was quick, but Jarod could feel the strength of the attacks and knew he could overpower Jordan. If he were not sparring Jarod might have laughed at the thought that he could overpower a Special Forces Officer. Six months ago he could barely pick up a sword.

The defensive sword forms he had never learned continued to flow through his mind. He had learned to accept them and follow as they led. Jordan paused slightly and the sword forms changed tactics for Jarod. He launched into the offensive against Jordan. With each stroke, Jarod added more power to his swings. Jordan's defensive blocks swayed farther to the sides with each of Jarod's strikes. As sword struck against sword, Jordan pulled a dagger and thrust it at Jarod chest. Jarod caught Jordan's wrist, and pulled it high and backwards, lifting Jordan off his feet and throwing him flat on his back. Jarod held Jordan's wrist to the ground with his knee and gently rested his sword on Jordan's exposed throat. He could apply slight pressure with his knee and break Jordan's hand, or apply pressure to his sword and do far worse.

Cheers and shouts rose from the crowd and Jarod felt his face flush. He hated being the center of attention. In school, the only time he had been the center of attention was when jokes were played on him. Usually it was from the town mayor's son, Billy Thompson, and his friends. Only recently had Jarod stood up against Billy and some of Billy's new army friends. Still, Jarod tried to keep his humility fresh every day. He had been given gifts that could give one's ego a dangerous boost and could easily lead one down treacherous paths.

Jarod looked into Jordan's eyes. "Are we done?"

Jordan swallowed. "Yes, Jarod. You have proven me wrong."

Jarod stood slowly as he held his sword. Some men would say anything to get revenge for having their egos squashed.

Jordan stood, sheathed his sword, and bowed to Jarod. Jarod bowed back, with his head up and his eyes facing Jordan. This was the opportunity that a person could use to hit his opponent on the back of the head. Jarod had already learned from his training that these circumstances could be fatal.

Jordan held out his hand. Jarod relaxed and shook the man's hand. Jordan studied Jarod for a second before speaking. "Well done, Jarod. Until today I have never met a man that could beat me in a duel, and today I have met three. Although I never sparred against them, it is safe to say that I would not want to oppose the weapons of Prince Daniel or Paladin Markos."

Jarod was stunned. "You know Paladin Markos?"

"I have just met him today. But after seeing him in person, I can believe the tales of his deeds."

Jarod grew hopeful. "Where might I find him? I have been entrusted by him with this child," Jarod said motioning to Thadius, "but we were separated during the siege."

"I am sorry Jarod. Paladin Markos has left on a mission to help find the Princess. That is our mission as well. Come, we have to make preparations."

Jarod's hopes fell. "I, unfortunately, must decline. As I have stated, I must watch over Thad until I can find Paladin Markos."

Jordan paused. "There are Sisters in the palace. I am sure they would take care of the child until you or Markos return."

Thad ran closer, held onto Jarod's hand and looked up at Jordan. "Is Sister Elizabeth there?" he asked excitedly.

"I am sorry, I am unaware of their names. But we can go and find out." Jordan looked at Jarod. "So?"

Events were rushing in on Jarod. He was being asked to go on a mission with Special Forces. He might find Sister, who could reunite Paladin Markos and Thadius. On the other hand, he would miss the little boy. But Thadius was not his little brother and he needed to be with his proper guardians. Jarod had also been given special talents, but his skills were not meant for babysitting. Jarod looked at Thad and smiled. Well, babysitting normal children that didn't run head long into an army of lizard creatures, anyway. He was being asked to go on a mission about a princess. He never knew there was a Princess of Rembelshem. But then again, he was only sixteen. He did not much care about politics.

"Okay. Let's meet the Sisters and make sure they know Paladin Markos."

Jordan looked at Jarod quizzically. "Jarod, everybody knows Paladin Markos."

"I didn't up until a few months back."

"I assure you. Any person in the armed forces, government, or related to the Paladins, knows of Paladin Markos." Jordan looked around the spectators. They all nodded their heads in agreement.

"Well, they must know him, not just know *of* him is what I am saying."

Jordan nodded. "Come then."

After saying their goodbyes and retrieving their belongings, Jarod and Thadius walked with Jordan toward Lansing.

"Jarod, can you carry me? I am getting tired," Thad asked.

"You? Getting tired? Are you feeling all right?"

"Just tired."

Jarod lifted Thadius unto his shoulders and continued walking next to Jordan.

Jordan looked at Jarod. "So, are you a Paladin?"

"A Paladin? No, no. I am not a Weapons Master either, as some say."

"Your talents seem like a Paladin's and you are watching the boy for Paladin Markos. I only assumed you might be a Paladin-in-training. So you can't heal others with prayer or such?"

Jarod was astonished by the statement. "Heal others with prayer? Is that possible?"

"Until today, I would not have thought it possible, but I know Paladin Markos healed Prince Daniel that way."

Jarod was deep in thought. He didn't know much about Paladins. He had been raised in a small northern town where fishing and logging were the most important activities. After this mission, he would search out the Paladins and get more information on the special gifts he had been given.

Jarod had only been in Lansing for less than an hour when he first met Thadius. Jarod had bought some clothes and had gone to the northern market on the outside of the twelve mile walls and the defensive ditch that surrounded the capital of Rembelshem. He and Thadius were then forced to flee to the Outlaw City once the Saurians attacked. Jarod had been forced to take care of the boy and protect him for the next few months.

Jarod looked at the city as they came nearer. He could see the three levels and the Royal Palace sitting in the very center of the city. Each of the three levels were raised twenty feet above the other, and each had a wall starting from the level before it and raising twenty feet above its foundation. Each level's wall circled its whole circumference. Each wall had soldiers twenty feet apart encompassing the whole twelve mile city.

Jordan led them across the southern bridge. It was one of only two bridges that led into the city over the twenty-foot wide and twenty-foot deep chasm that surrounded the entire city. At the back of the ditch began the outer walls of the city. The walls began at the bottom of the ditch and rose twenty feet above ground level.

Jarod studied the bridge as they walked across. Instead of a normal drawbridge, the bridge was designed such that in the event of an attack, the middle of the bridge would split and drop all invaders into the defensive ditch. Jarod shuddered as he remembered the siege of Lansing, and all the lizard creatures and humans alike that fell to their deaths.

Jarod had never been in the Southern Business District, but it looked similar to its northern counterpart. Shops, inns, and taverns lined the outside wall in both directions. The outer wall to the second level started three hundred feet in from the city entrance. Buildings were only allowed on the outer wall of the city so that no structure could be used defensively by an invading force. The thin, three-hundred foot business district would not allow a large force to attack all at once, and those that entered would be easily targeted by the archers walking on the second level walls.

As he entered the city, Jarod was once again amazed by the fast pace of the city. Each person moved busily from one store to another. He had been slightly overwhelmed the first time he had entered the city, but he was more prepared this time. The number of people in this one little section was more than were in his small home town of Kalkaska.

Jordan continued to lead them through the business district and toward the second level entrance. As he stood at the base of the marble stairs leading to the second level, Jarod stared at the enormous silver statues standing on the entrance of the second level. Jarod had seen the statues from a distance as they walked into the business district, but being closer to them now revealed just how tall and dangerous they really were. The statues stood at the base of the second level, blocking any large carts or war equipment that might try to pass through. Jarod knew from his studies that the statues were also electrically grounded by an underground room. In the event of an attack, the grounding mechanism could be removed, and the statues could release enough of a shock to kill an elephant if they were to be touched. The paranoia of the previous Lancaster Kings was mentioned in school studies, but there was something about actually seeing the defensive measures put in place to keep intruders from reaching the central castle.

The second level was the Residential District. Houses lined the maze of roads as far as Jarod could see. Jarod swallowed. He had been with the army, but the number of residents living on the second level was overwhelming. A person could easily get lost in the maze of roads. He continued to follow Jordan, who seemed to know where he was heading.

They finally reached a main road that led straight up to the stairs of the Royal Level. Jarod figured they were about a half mile from the Royal Level. The Royal Palace stood like a white beacon in the sunshine. It was hard for him to believe he was actually going to enter the historic building. Never in his life would he have imagined himself going to the Royal Palace of Rembelshem, let alone invited.

The closer they came to the Royal Level, the larger and nicer the houses became. The houses closest to the Royal Level were the size of two or three inns combined. The stairs leading to the Royal Palace

Level were marble, just like the second level entrance. The outer third level wall was similar to the other levels and stretched from the second level to ten feet higher than the base of the third level. More archers patrolled the wall surrounding the Royal Level.

Even larger houses stood to his right next to the outer wall. But beyond them and to his left were open grass plains mixed with forests and gardens. Once they drew closer to the palace he could see a lake to the left of the palace, and a moat encircling the castle. Two defensive drawbridges were on opposite sides of the entrance, allowing carts to be pulled in one side and out the other. The ceiling of the entrance was forty feet high. Two large spiraling staircases rose on either side, leading to the eastern or western towers of the castle.

Jarod was astonished. Never in his life had he seen such luxurious decorations and design. The entryway and the stairs leading to the towers were both made of white marble.

"Jarod?" Jordan called.

Jarod found himself mesmerized by the surroundings. He had stopped traffic coming into the palace. He blushed, then caught up with Jordan. He lifted Thad from his shoulders.

"It will probably be more proper if you walk by yourself in here," Jarod said to Thadius.

"The Sisters are usually on the second story of the east tower if they are not patrolling," Jordan said, guiding Jarod to the stairs.

"Patrolling?"

"For the lizard creatures. There are those that can see the creatures for what they are, but most of us cannot. It is said the Sisters are gifted with the sword similar to how the Paladins are gifted." Jordan shrugged. "The Sisters are supposedly equal in skill to my Special Forces." Jordan paused at the marble steps and studied Jarod for a second. "After today, I think I might have to reconsider my attitude, though. Come, we have a busy day to get ready for our mission."

Jarod thought to himself that it would be busy only *if* he felt comfortable in leaving Thadius with the Sisters.

"Sister Elizabeth!" Thadius squealed and ran from the top of the steps toward two ladies dressed in white armor.

"Thadius?" the younger sister said, kneeling and giving Thad a hug. "Where have you been?"

"I've been with Jarod," Thadius's said excitedly as he pointed to Jarod.

Sister Elizabeth lifted her head toward to the two approaching men. Jarod felt uncomfortable under the Sister's gaze. The younger sister stood and studied him momentarily while the older one squinted at him.

Jordan stepped ahead of Jarod. "Sisters, it is my pleasure to introduce Jarod the Great."

Jarod blushed. He was not ready to be introduced by that name to somebody in the Sister's position.

"Just Jarod, please. It is a pleasure to meet you," Jarod said, bowing to the sisters.

"Jarod the Great? But you are just a boy," the older sister said.

"I assure you Sister, he is as I say. I doubted as well, but I was taught a lesson in humility today."

She raised an eyebrow.

"Jarod the Great?" Sister Elizabeth raised a

hand to her mouth. "Thadius, was that you who broke the siege?"

Thad was not sure what the question meant. Sister Elizabeth looked to Jarod. He nodded his head.

"Thank you, Jarod for watching Thadius. When Paladin Markos returns I am sure he will want to meet you. He has been very worried about young Thadius."

"Yes, he will be interested in meeting you for more than one reason," the older sister said as she continued studying him. "I do not recognize you Jarod. Did you study under a Paladin?"

"No, ma'am. Why?"

"Your presence is strong, almost blinding. More so than most Paladins. You don't understand, do you?"

Jarod shook his head.

"Paladin Markos will explain when you meet him."

Jordan stepped in. "For now, Sisters, Jarod and I are tasked with a mission of our own. Hopefully Jarod will have the pleasure of meeting Paladin Markos then." Jordan looked at Jarod. "That is, I assume you are comfortable with the arrangements for the young boy to be watched?"

"Yes. If the Sisters can watch Thadius until I or Paladin Markos returns?" Jarod asked.

Sister Elizabeth spoke first. "It would be our pleasure to have the company of Thadius again."

"Sisters, if you will excuse us," Jordan said with a bow.

The two sisters exchanged glances, but then looked at Jarod once again and bowed back.

Jarod kneeled in front of Thad. "I am going to be gone for a little while. When I get back, I'll come find you. Stay with the Sisters and behave yourself. And don't eat all of the palace food, ok?"

Thad smiled. "Just all their pancakes."

Jarod smiled and gave Thad a hug. Jarod stood and bowed to the sisters. "Sisters."

Jordan turned and led Jarod up the stairs.

"Do you have any clue about what they were talking about?" Jarod asked.

"None. Their kind and my kind do not usually associate with one another, if you know what I mean."

Jarod did. He had spent a few months with the army, so he knew how they acted and talked.

Jarod looked up as they climbed the stairs. The circular path of the stairs allowed him to look all the way to the top of the castle. The fifteen foot marble steps circled clockwise with each rotation ending at the level above. This created a twenty-foot opening in the middle of the stairs with a view straight to the top of the palace.

They climbed three flights of the winding stairs before Jordan led Jarod down a hallway. "We'll get you equipped first, and then meet the rest of the team."

Jordan unlocked a door and led Jarod into a room. "This is the Special Forces armory." Jordan walked to an open closet of black outfits and turned to look at Jarod. Jordan sized up Jarod and turned back to pull a uniform from the closet. "I think this should fit."

Jordan handed Jarod the black chain mail mesh. Jarod held it up to look at it. It looked very familiar. The chain mail was coated in a black rubber substance and there were black leather shoulder and arm pads on it. It was the same uniform that the inn-keeper, Daniel Smith, had worn when they first started out on their journey from their destroyed village to the capital.

"Shielded chain mail. Nothing worse than crawling on your belly to sneak up on a target, losing grounding from your boots and getting zapped in the chest by regular chain mail."

Jarod nodded. He understood the implications. The bullies from school used to pull his grounding boots off and touch him with metal objects.

"One or two swords?"

"Huh?" Jarod replied.

Jordan lifted two scabbards. A one-sword scabbard to fit on a belt, and a two-sword holder that could be worn over the chest with the swords held on the wearers back.

"If the rumors are true, then you are more proficient with two swords than most."

"Two swords, please," Jarod said, forcing himself not to smile. If Daniel Smith could see him now. The irony of being offered a two sword scabbard was funny. A year ago, he could barely lift one sword. Now he was more proficient with two swords than most, and he was being offered a scabbard like the Weapons Master Mr. Smith had worn on their journey together.

"I'll be right back. Just need to check to see where the team is. You can change in here."

Jarod changed into the new armor and was able to figure out how to strap the double scabbard on his back and around his chest. He was thankful Jordan had stepped away, as he had looked rather foolish during the process of figuring it out.

A knock came at the door and Jordan peeked his head in. "You ready?"

"Yes, Sir."

Jarod walked out and Jordan locked the door behind him. Jordan led Jarod down the same hall, but away from the stairs. "I talked to the team and it seems you have already met most of them."

Jordan turned and led Jarod through an open door and into a mess hall. Six men with armor similar to Jarod's sat at a table. They turned their heads toward Jarod. He could not believe who sat at the table. Five of the men were the Special Forces members who had challenged him while he was with the army. The sixth man was the worst of all. It was Billy Thompson, his old bully from school.

"I am starting to believe that there are no coincidences when you are involved," Jordan said.

Jarod sighed and looked at Jordan. "Me too."

CHAPTER SIX
The Arc'Reisheen Decree

"The government is merely a servant -- merely a temporary servant; it cannot be its prerogative to determine what is right and what is wrong, and decide who is a patriot and who isn't. Its function is to obey orders, not originate them." - Mark Twain (1835 - 1910)

THE SAURIAN QUEEN pulled her cloak closer around her as she walked through the forest. Even though the sun shone high in the noon sky, the shade of the trees gave her chills. She would have preferred to meet in the open under the warmth of the sun, but the voice was adamant against it. It was nice, however, to get away from the camp and the filth of untrained slaves. She detested the fact that her people needed to live on the planet's surface, but their technology, which had kept them safe for so long, was barely functioning deep within the Earth. She was forced to have her people leave their underground sanctuary and move into the savagery of the human world.

She was the Avent'Antar, the Saurian Queen, and her legacy would mark her as the queen who was forced to lead her people to the outer world. Her title and memories were passed down to her from her genetic donors, but none before her had gone through such events. The voice had led her through the past ten years in preparation for the battle against the humans, and her people's exile from their underground caverns. An idea that she was afraid to admit would not have come to her until much later if she had been on her own. The voice had led her to control three fourths of this particular continent, and it had yet to be wrong in its decision-making. This bothered the Avent'Antar.

It was illogical that there was a being higher in intelligence and ability than she and her people. But the voice was there. She could not detect it in any form. The dragons had similar abilities, but were un-intelligent animals. As instructed, she had advised the strongest of abilities in her army to study the dragons and their ability to bend the light. They had learned the secrets but could not find the dragons again. The dragons were unknown to her people. Could there be more intelligent species that had also remained hidden for so long?

Do not fret yourself over what you cannot comprehend, Saurian Queen. There is more hidden in this world than any of your people could ever imagine. The feminine voice invaded the queen's mind. *The end of the human occupation of the lands is close. You are proceeding as instructed?*

Yes. The army is regrouping and preparing for the

final battle against what is left of the humans. They are spread so vast, will they really join as one army against us?

You doubt me? The voice asked irritatably. *They will join together as I have foretold. You hold their leaders as the key. But the human race will never bond as one and will be easily defeated as they continue to squabble amongst themselves. Your victory is assured, Saurian Queen.*

"My apologies," the Avent'Antar said out loud accidentally. The voice treated her as if she were no better than a human. The queen regained her composure.

The humans will send many to free your captives. Guard them well.

The queen bowed. *Until the next time.*

* * * *

IZIKAR'ETRA SANDAMUNG'SO waited at the edge of the forest to which he had escorted the Avent'Antar. This was the third time in the last month she had visited the woods alone without explanation. The woods were cold and damp, and it seemed illogical one of his kind would willingly go there. It was not his job to question the queen, but it was his job to protect his people. He was the Arc'Reisheen, the second-in-command of the Saurian army, and his loyalties were to the people and not to the queen or the council. Ever since the days of the uprising against the previous Avent'Antar genetic lineage, the Arc'Reisheen had been given an order to secretly monitor the queen and the council. The Arc'Reisheen Decree was unknown to any but those receiving the genetic makeup to become the next Arc'Reisheen.

There was movement in the bushes on the outskirts of the forest, then the movement subsided. He waited a few seconds, then three Psi'Drakor appeared in front of him. The Psi'Drakors looked the same as other Saurians, but their mental abilities allowed them their special position. The three currently wore the Saurian Special Forces silver spiked armor and helms.

"Report," Izikar stated.

One stepped forward and bowed. "Arc'Reisheen, we cannot confirm the Avent'Antar was meeting with an individual. Although it seemed she was possibly communicating with somebody tele-pathically. It cannot be confirmed."

Izikar nodded. "Take guard position."

The three Saurian Special Forces once again used their abilities to bend the light and disappear from normal sight. They would continue to provide security as hidden guards to the Izikar and the queen as they walked back to camp.

The queen emerged from the forest and paused to absorb the warmth of the sun. She then proceeded to walk past Izikar toward the camp. The Arc'Reisheen took his position, following behind her on the right side. He would continue watching her as a guard, and also fulfilling the Arc'Reisheen Creed. If the queen chose a path that lead the people into harm, he would be forced to step in. The last uprising was a tragic civil war. He hoped it would never come to that again.

* * * *

EKRA WATCHED the invisible guards lead the foolish queen toward their camp. Divide and conquer. The humans were split and now the seed of doubt had been planted in the Saurians. All was going as planned.

* * * *

A KNOCK CAME from the outside of Izikar's tent.

Come, Izikar thought to the visitor.

A female Saurian in a long blue dress opened the door covering and entered Izikar's tent.

Are you alone?

Izikar nodded.

"Arc'Reisheen," the female Saurian began with a bow, "it has been brought to our attention that the human currently in charge of the Rembelshem country wishes to obtain a private meeting with a Saurian leader. We currently hold his daughter and brother and he wishes to make arrangements for their release."

"What are the conditions of the meeting?" Izikar asked.

"A location of your choice and only with him, the Saurian in command, and the mediator who contacted him."

"Return tomorrow and I will have a location for the meeting," Izikar said.

The female Saurian bowed. "It should also be noted, that this human leader is one that is somehow protected and cannot be deceived by our illusions. It is not known whether these humans can see your Psi-Drakors yet."

Izikar nodded and the Saurian left the tent.

"Do we follow?" a hidden voice questioned from behind Izikar.

"No. We will deal with the Human Sympathizers later. Our primary goal will be to capture a human who has gained the ability to guard their minds against us. It may be true they can see you. I have seen first-hand that the humans have acquired weapons and skills that we are not aware of. We will plan accordingly."

CHAPTER SEVEN
Jarod the Great!?

"All the world is a stage,

And all the men and women merely players.

They have their exits and entrances;

Each man in his time plays many part"

-William Shakespeare (1564 - 1616)

DANIEL RAN HIS HANDS through his hair. He sat at his desk looking through the Rembelshem daily reports and the other government documents that needed his signature. There were multiple reasons why he never cared to acquire a political position, and this was one of them. The paperwork for running his small inn used to take him less than an hour, which left him plenty of time for the more important duty of being a father. If circumstances had been different, and he and Hannah had stayed to raise Rebekah in the palace, he would never have seen his family.

The thought of his wife created a brief image of her. He struggled to hold the image in his mind for a bit longer, but it faded away. Daniel swallowed at the heartache it caused. It had been sixteen years since Hannah had died during Rebekah's birth, but the pain was still there.

"I need to go for a walk," Daniel said.

Phillip Smith leaned back in a large burgundy chair and reviewed government papers. "Rebekah?"

"Hannah. I have more memories of Hannah in the palace than anywhere else. Around every corner I have images of places I had seen her. I never had to deal with that in my inn."

Daniel's old teacher nodded. "Come, this can wait. Others might not think so, but the country will not stop if you are an hour late. Let's head down to the gardens. It is best to enjoy what flowers are left before the snow begins to fall."

Daniel grabbed his black cloak from a hook on the wall. The autumn weather had begun, and the cool winds brought a hint of snow. Daniel waited for Phillip to put on his own cloak, then they headed out of the study.

Outside the room the eight King's Guards snapped to attention and positioned themselves around the prince and his teacher. Daniel began walking down the hallway toward the stairs. They reached the third level landing as The General stepped off the stairs.

"Ah, Prince Daniel, I was just coming to see you," came the dark man's deep, grated voice. "Most of the scouts have returned. The Saurians control the southern regions of all the nations. We assume they will wait until after the snow is gone to attack the northern regions."

The General coughed and a small mimicking cough resounded from the hallway behind Daniel.

"Cold?"

The big man nodded.

"Position half the army at the Great Wall and the other half will rotate as interior and exterior defense for Lansing. Hopefully the lizard creatures do not like the cold as we suspect, and they will wait until spring. That should give us enough time to prepare."

"Yes, your Highness," the General said, ending with another cough. The small mimicking cough resounded again. The General smiled as he looked toward the sound. "Excuse me, your Highness."

Daniel watched as the giant man stood straight and adjusted his armor. The King's Guards were nearly seven feet tall, but the General was their height and a hundred pounds of muscle more. The big man puffed up his chest and took large dramatic strides toward a young blonde child being followed by two of the Sisters.

The General's deep voice resounded in the

hallway as he spoke. "Who dares mock me? Why, I should squash you like a tiny grape," he bellowed as he pounded his fist into his open palm.

The little boy waved his hand with a smile. "Oooh, ooh, me, me."

The General laughed and looked up at the ceiling. "I'll squash you later. The ceiling is too low in here."

"Oh, coocooberries!" the blonde child said with a frown.

Daniel smiled at the exchange of words, then he paused at the child's remark. *Coocooberries* was a word he and Rebekah had made up, and as far as he knew, was only known to them. Daniel broke away from the guards and headed back to the child.

Daniel bowed. "Sisters." Daniel turned his attention to the young boy. "Do you know the Princess, young one? Maybe you know her as Rebekah?" Daniel asked.

The boy gave a big smile. "Is Rebekah here? Uncle Markos said we could see her."

Uncle Markos? Things were not adding up, but now the boy seemed familiar. Daniel's mind raced.

He tried to put the pieces together, then it finally occurred to him who the boy was.

"You are the boy Jarod watched for Paladin Markos?"

The boys smile grew even larger and he nodded. "Yes, Jarod the Great."

Daniel thought back to the scrawny teenager he had begun training and he chuckled. "No, his name is Jarod O'Grady."

Thadius's face grew serious. "No, he is Jarod the Great."

"No you must have gotten confused with the names, he is definitely not Jarod the Great."

"Prince Daniel, we met the young man and had our doubts as well, but Special Forces Officer Jordan was confident that the boy watching over Thadius was indeed the rumored Jarod the Great. He has recently left with Jordan of the Special Forces and relinquished care of Thadius until he or Paladin Markos returns," Sister Elizabeth said.

Daniel paused in a stupor. His brain seemed to stop as the horror crashed in on him. The thin gangly teen he had protected from their home town, who could barely lift a sword, was now imitating a Weapons Master. He had left with the Special Forces to retrieve Rebekah. He was putting the lives of those men and his daughter in jeopardy by pretending to be somebody he was not. Daniel had given him the only training he had ever had, and the boy was barely able to handle that.

"I will kill him," Daniel blurted out.

"Prince Daniel?" Sister Elizabeth questioned.

"When I get my hands on his scrawny neck," Daniel said, his temper rising. "He is putting on an act. I know the boy. He is from where Rebekah and I have been living. I brought him to Lansing and trained him in what little he knows."

Daniel took a deep breath and looked down at Thadius. "I am sorry, I will not actually *kill* Jarod. I am just upset."

Thadius grabbed Daniel's hand and patted it with another. "It is alright. I wouldn't want you to try and hurt Jarod. You would get hurt."

"I…" Daniel began.

"Come Thadius, we need to see the doctor," Sister Elizabeth interjected.

"Is everything alright?" the General asked in a worried tone.

"He has been tired lately and not feeling well. The doctor keeps trying different remedies but nothing has worked yet. Hopefully Paladin Markos will be back soon."

"Use any resources from the palace that you need to make him better," Daniel said.

"Thank you, Prince Daniel. Hopefully it is just allergies or a minor cold."

Daniel bowed to the Sisters and watched as they descended the stairs.

"OK, forget the garden, who wants to go spar? Want to join, General?"

The big man laughed. "A chance to challenge a Weapons Master? Definitely."

* * * *

DANIEL RUBBED his sore chin. The General was faster than he expected for such a big man. Daniel learned that the big man's punches were as powerful as one would expect. In the end, Daniel was forced to use his legs to perform a choke hold against the man.

Daniel sat back at his desk as Phillip continued to review the papers he had left previously.

"Your Higness?" a female voice said from the far corner of the room.

Daniel jumped up and held a sword toward the voice. A Saurian female stood at the opposite side of his study. From the dress it looked like the same one that had contacted him before. But they may all wear the same outfits for all he knew.

Phillip stood and studied the Saurian. "Same one?"

Daniel nodded.

The Saurian ignored Phillip. "Your Highness, I bring new information regarding your daughter."

"Continue," Daniel responded.

"Our leaders would like to offer a trade; your daughter for the release of our soldiers that you took prisoner during the battle for this city."

Daniel forced himself not to accept the offer. "We will provide fifty Saurian soldiers for the release of my daughter and the other fifty for the release of my brother."

The Saurian walked slowly to the open window and sat on the ledge. Daniel watched as the creature relished the sun light, then turned its attention back to him.

"That is acceptable. I will return with information about this meeting and the prisoner trade."

The female Saurian leaned back and fell out the window. Phillip rushed to the window and peered out.

"It's gone."

Daniel nodded knowingly. "After this next meeting, make sure bars are placed on all the windows."

CHAPTER EIGHT
Duke Run!

"The best remedy for those who are afraid, lonely or unhappy is to go outside, somewhere where they can be quiet, alone with the heavens, nature and God. Because only then does one feel that all is as it should be and that God wishes to see people happy, amidst the simple beauty of nature." - Anne Frank (1929 - 1945)

MARKOS PATTED the big horse's neck. "What do you think, Duke? Go slowly? Yes, it is new territory and I should tread cautiously. But, nevertheless, I hope you are not too mad. It has been only you and I for so long. This new path with Sister Elizabeth is scary, though. I get more nervous around her than around anything we have ever come across."

Markos led the big, dark brown horse by the reins over the rocky mountain pass. The tall evergreen trees blocked most of the harsh cold wind, but Markos's face still stung from the bitter cold. The dusting of snow that covered the ground forced Markos to cautiously watch where Duke walked. They were headed down from the mountain, and it would warm up by the end of the day as they made their way to the lower altitudes.

Markos paused to listen, but it was too late when he heard the sound of rock grating against rock. He yelled in pain as a human-sized boulder rolled and bound his ankle against the ground.

Markos lay on his back and took deep breaths, trying to shut out the pain. He grimaced from the pain as he tried to pull his ankle free. The boulder was solid and there was no way he could move it in his current position.

It would snow during the night, and he could probably make it through until morning, but by then he would have used most of his energy to keep from freezing to death. Unless help came, which was unlikely in this part of the mountains, his chances of survival looked bleak.

Markos could still feel his large two-headed axe in the scabbard on his back. He lifted his body slightly, removed the axe and placed it on his chest. He lay back down and closed his eyes to think. There really was no other option, die or lose his foot. Markos sighed and then abruptly opened his eyes.

"You have been waiting for this chance to catch me helpless haven't you?"

Markos could feel the unseen evil surrounding him. Five of them slowly circling and advancing toward him. Duke whinnied.

"I know, I know," Markos said in response.

There was no way he could fight them in his current position. His choice had been made. He only hoped he could endure the pain long enough for Duke to carry him down the mountain. Markos sat up and hefted his axe against his palm. He bent his right leg back to gain more stability to swing from his awkward position. He hoped he could supply enough force to take only one swing.

Markos sensed the creatures closing in on him faster. He had killed so many of their kind. He could only guess they had waited for such a day and now relished the chance for retribution. Markos flexed his hand around the axe and took deep breaths. He raised the axe above his head. Suddenly, a new sensation stopped him and he looked in the direction from where he sensed it. *This isn't even funny.* He knew the sensation. It had haunted and chased him most of his life. He could not see it but he knew the dragon was close.

"Duke, home!" Markos yelled.

At the sound of the command, the big horse ran into the woods. Markos knew Duke would have stayed to fight the dragon, but it would have been a futile battle.

As he watched Duke run, the snow-covered evergreens and the horse were suddenly blocked by a huge red body standing over him.

The dragon's body was covered by silk-like, fist-sized scales that switched from purple to red as the creature moved and tensed its muscles. Each of the four legs surrounding Markos were almost as tall and wide as he was, and its body was slightly larger than an elephant. The creature arched its neck and breathed a half circle stream of fire into the trees in front of it.

Markos grabbed his shield that lay next to him and covered his head and body. He thought his face and hands might blister from the tremendous heat that bathed him. He did not know if the shield would protect him against a direct blast, but the shield was covered with the same type of scales that seemed to protect the dragon.

Markos could not see. He was forced to cover his ears as the creature released a low-pitched roar that caused the rocky ground beneath Markos to tremble. Suddenly, all was quiet. Markos could still feel the dragon and could hear it drawing in large breaths. He could feel the dragon's snout run across his leg. He braced for the worst. He knew the shield would not protect him from the dragon's jaws. The dragon continued up to the shield Markos held, and then…it *sniffed him*? Markos peered around his shield and looked directly at a head-sized eye.

"Be gone you evil beast!" Markos yelled.

Evil?

Markos was confused. The voice in his head was not his own. The dragon stepped back and opened its jaws. Markos grabbed his axe. It would not do much, but he would do what he could.

"If it is time to finish the course, then come you foul thing. I have fought the good fight and I have kept the faith."

The dragon paused, its head over Markos, and puffed hot air from its nose at Markos's head. The dragon opened its jaws over the boulder and flung it into trees. It crashed into the evergreens, then into the ground.

Evil? Foul? You compare me to those things that were ready to attack you? A male voice said in Markos's mind.

"I, um," Markos paused and looked at the dragon as it stared at him. "Are you talking to me?"

I have always figured you to be smarter than that. Of course, I am talking to you. Now get moving, my bluff was called and those things are coming back.

Markos had been distracted, but now he could sense the creatures returning. He carefully stood up, but he could not put any weight on the foot that had been stuck under the boulder. He put his axe in his back scabbard and picked up his shield. The only thing he could do was hop on one leg. Without Duke, he would never get away.

That will not work. The dragon dropped to its belly. *Get on my back.*

"Excuse me? Are you crazy?"

No, my mentality is fine. You have no other choice. I can carry you away, or you can deal with whatever those things are. If I wanted you dead, you would be dead. Now get on.

Markos looked at the dragon. It was true. If the beast had wanted to kill him, he would have been eaten already.

Eating humans is forbidden. Humans have a toxin in their bodies that poisons us.

"You can read my thoughts?"

Yes, you do not have to speak out loud to converse. It is a waste of energy.

"That is rather disconcerting. I will speak out loud if you don't mind."

Your choice. Now get on or I am leaving.

The dragon's waist was the lowest to the ground, so Markos was able to climb on there.

Now climb up and grab my neck.

Markos climbed up. The dragon's scales were just like his armor – smooth and cool. He reached the dragon's back and was barely able to clasp his wrist around its huge neck.

Hold on.

The dragon leaped into the air and flapped its great wings. Markos squeezed the dragon's neck tighter. If he had known it was going to fly he would never have gotten on its back! But the dragon began to move forward over the treetops and Markos changed his mind. The sight was amazing! He had always wished to fly like the birds or the ancients in their flying devices, and now here he was, looking at the ground rushing past him from the air.

Hang on, you will like this even more.

Markos had forgotten the dragon could read his thoughts. The dragon flapped its wings harder and they rose higher into the sky. The dragon tilted its body and maneuvered toward a group of tall, snow-covered mountain peaks. As he reached the peaks, the dragon dove into the valley beyond. The great mountains rushed by on both sides. The dragon climbed again and headed for a small gap in between two mountains. The gap was too small for the dragon to make it through with its wings, and Markos was squeezing its neck harder. When it reached the gap, the dragon folded its wings next to its body and let its velocity carry it through.

Markos could not help but release an adrenaline-filled shout of joy.

The dragon circled back toward the two peaks and slowly descended until he grasped the top of the mountain.

Markos looked over the Earth from the top of the world. To the east he could see the lands break from the mountains into the autumn brown, and the green vegetation grew to the south.

"My God, my God, your artwork is more majestic than any could imagine."

The dragon released its grip and fell backwards, then turned its head into a dive. It flew south, then lowered itself into a clearing in a hardwoods forest. It settled to the ground, then allowed Markos to slide off its back.

Markos hopped on his good leg and leaned against a tree. He looked at the dragon.

"Thank you. You saved my life and showed me things I have dreamed of seeing. But I do not understand why. Have you not tracked me all my life?"

I have watched you many times. I have seen you fight the invisible creatures more than once. I cannot see them, but I can smell and feel their evil presence. You have never been as vulnerable as you were today, and I could not watch you die. I feel a bond with you, whereas I do not with any other human. And now you wear the skin of a dragon on your clothes. A dragon from my lineage judging by the smell. This is not possible. When a dragon dies, it returns to the energy of the universe, and no part is left behind. Tell me how you have acquired this skin?

"This armor was once my father's. I do not know from whom he received it. My father and mother were killed by a dragon."

Impossible! It is forbidden to kill humans. None of my kind would dare break such a sacred rule.

"I have met one dragon that tried to kill my father and me. Only by this shield," Markos said tapping his shield, "did we survive."

The dragon knocked over some trees as it stomped its foot and swung its tail. *After I have broken the rules to save you, you speak such lies to me?*

"I do not lie. As a child, my father took me to a cave where we found men destroying dragon eggs. My father fought the men, but only one egg survived. A parent dragon came back into the cave to find my father and me standing around the broken eggs. It thought we were the ones who broke the eggs, so it blew fire at us. Only from behind this shield did we survive."

All my siblings were killed by humans. Since my hatching, the eyes of a human child are my first memory. Was that you?

The question brought memories back to Markos. His father fighting against the men. The one remaining egg cracking, revealing intelligent eyes that stared at him from within the shell.

Markos swallowed. "Yes, yes, it was I."

CHAPTER NINE
Chosen

"You gain strength, courage and confidence by every experience in which
you really stop to look fear in the face. You are able to say to yourself, 'I
have lived through this horror. I can take the next thing that comes
along.' You must do the thing you think you cannot do." - Eleanor
Roosevelt (1884 - 1962)

ROBERT LOOKED at his niece in disgust. "How can you be so happy?"

"Happy about being in a slave camp in which the enemy or many of the captives would not think twice about killing me?" Rebekah paused and leaned on her shovel. "I have to have faith that I am here for a reason."

Robert took another swing at the ground with his pick axe. He was getting more proficient using only his left hand for laborious work. He would have used both hands if he still had his right arm. Rebekah shoveled the rocks and dirt from the hole her uncle had dug and put them in the wagon next to her.

"Foolish nonsense. To think a God would allow his follower to be enslaved and treated like an animal. We sit here and dig houses for our enemies. How does that benefit anyone?" Robert asked.

Rebekah shrugged. "Whether I go through good or bad times, there is always one constant in my life. I focus on that constant and pray I will someday know the reasons for my struggles."

The King shook his head. "It's strange that your father, one of the most dangerous men in the country, taught you such things. I even feared for my life when he was still in the castle. He has always wanted the throne."

"Unlike you who killed my mother and almost me?"

Robert threw his pick axe to the ground and struck an aggressive pose toward Rebekah. "As I told you before, Princess, that is a story your father must have told you so that you would want to kill me. I had nothing to do with your mother's death."

Rebekah held her shovel defensively. "My father had nothing to do with me being captured by you. That was all your doing. You were also the one who hoarded the food from the citizens of Lansing."

A whip snapped close to Robert and Rebekah. "Get back to work," a Saurian guard shouted, ready to strike at one of them.

Robert reached down and retrieved his axe. Rebekah began digging again. The guard waited a few minutes, then moved on. Neither spoke to the other for the rest of their work shift.

The horn blew. It was time for the prisoners to go back to their cages. Rebekah hated dinner time.

The slop the Saurians provided was barely edible. It seemed to satisfy their body's need for protein and substance, but that was about it. She could deal with the hard work and the harsh living environment, but it would be more tolerable with some decent food.

Rebekah took her bowl of food and returned to her cage. Saurian guards were stationed twenty feet apart along the long line of wooden cells. Rebekah had already seen one prisoner try to run. He was killed instantly by something Rebekah could not see. She shuddered as the image of the man being killed flashed through her mind. Anybody who had seen the incident would not run anytime soon.

"Princess?"

Rebekah swallowed and gripped her spoon tighter. The female Saurian approached Rebekah and sat down close to her.

The Saurian reached out with her scaly hand. "My name is Della."

Rebekah looked at the Saurian and raised an eyebrow.

"You poor thing. You have been working too hard. You still think I am one of them?"

"I know you are one of them. You can stop the facade," Rebekah said harshly.

Della squinted looking at Rebekah.

"Then what am I wearing?" Della asked.

Rebekah looked at the Saurian.

"You're wearing a long, light blue dress that has a gold collar and cuffs. It has intricate gold embroidering down the front as well."

Rebekah chuckled as she saw the Saurian's eyes widen with surprise.

"But, but...." Della paused, "we have heard rumors about some humans that have evolved enough to block our illusions. You must be one of those few."

"No, it is because of a higher power that protects me from your tricks."

"As in a god? That is illogical."

Rebekah shrugged. "Believe what you want. I see all of you for what you are. Except for whatever killed that man yesterday. Do you see it?"

Rebekah was surprised to see the Saurian turn a shade whiter.

Della shook her head. "They are the Psi'Drakor. None of us can see them. Their abilities are different than the normal illusions we use against you humans. They somehow bend the light around themselves so that if you look at them all you see is what is behind them. No mind tricks, just pure scientific invisibility. It is beyond your comprehension."

Rebekah forgot how arrogant the Saurians were. To the Saurians, humans seemed to rank just slightly higher than animals.

She now knew what the hidden weapon was beyond the outskirts of the camp. She had run into them before, these Psi'Drakor. They were the ones who had spied on her and helped capture her in the palace.

She had one question answered. Maybe she could get more.

"So why is it that you are held prisoner?" Rebekah asked.

"I am part of a group who disagrees with the Queen about the treatment of humans. The war is a must, but we don't believe that all of you should be killed. For my punishment, I am forced to live with you humans."

More prisoners entered the jail cell. King Robert entered and sat on the other side of Rebekah. She knew he would rather not be by her, but she was the lesser of two evils. He had the choice of the Dangarian and Republic citizens – lifetime enemies of his – or the niece who had cut off his arm.

A horn that Rebekah did not recognize blew in the distance. The guards lining the cells stood to attention. Rebekah noticed Della flinching and shrinking closer to the cell bars.

"What is it?" Rebekah asked.

"The Queen."

"I finally get to see this queen of yours."

Rebekah noticed her uncle looking at her strangely.

"Referring to the Saurians," Rebekah said, nodding her head at the guards while trying to cover up Della's secret.

A progression of Saurian guards marched past the jail cells. At each jail cell they paused for half a minute, then moved forward. Rebekah finally saw the infamous queen that the Saurians worshipped. The queen sat on a covered sedan chair, carried by four human males in white garb. She wore a long, white, gold embroidered dress with a matching two-foot high headpiece.

The men carrying the queen's chariot stopped in front of Rebekah's cell as the queen slowly studied the occupants. Her gaze fixed on Della, then shifted to Rebekah. The queen said something in the Saurian language and pointed to Rebekah. The guards opened the gate and rushed in, grabbing Rebekah by the arms and carrying her over to the Saurian Queen. Rebekah struggled to break her arms free, but the two soldiers were far stronger.

The queen studied Rebekah closer, grinned, then looked back at Della. The queen motioned the guards forward and Rebekah was forced to go with them. Rebekah could hear the taunts of the Dangarian Prince and his friends as she was carried away.

* * * *

REBEKAH WAS BROUGHT to the largest tent in the encampment. The tent was filled with luxurious human furniture and ornaments. Rebekah had no idea what many of the items were. A soldier holding her arm kicked the back of her knee and forced her to kneel on the ground.

Another soldier stepped through a drape in the back of the tent and held it open as the queen stepped through. The queen walked over and stood in front of Rebekah. A human female clothed in a plain, long white dress and white headpiece brought the queen a steaming drink. The queen motioned. The servant positioned herself against the wall.

"You are the Princess of Rembelshem, yes?" the Saurian Queen asked.

"Yes," Rebekah answered. They obviously knew who she was. There was no sense in lying about it.

"Good, you tell the truth." The queen said. She nodded to the guard to her right. The guard stuck his dirty, scaly fingers into Rebekah's mouth, baring her gums. "You seem to have all your teeth and your health is good compared to most of your species. You will do nicely as my first uplander servant," the queen said. She motioned to the female next to the wall.

Rebekah looked at the servant. The job sounded far better than shoveling rocks and dirt. Plus, if it got her close to the queen, she might be able to end this war.

"What do I need to do?"

"You will need to be trained and swear allegiance to me."

Rebekah was distraught. The job sounded nicer than the one she had, but to swear allegiance to the Saurian Queen went against everything she believed. She would rather dig holes.

"Thank you for the opportunity, but I must pass."

"Young Princess, it was never a question of *if* you would. You will be my servant." The queen looked at the guard to Rebekah's right. "Begin the process."

The guards dragged Rebekah to a ten-foot high wooden pole standing in one of the open squares. They forced Rebekah's back against the pole and locked her around the pole with metal cuffs. Rebekah's mind raced. She looked for a way out, but there was none.

Two guards lifted her off the ground, while two others removed her grounding boots. She tried to kick, but they had her legs locked. Rebekah looked up to see another soldier carrying a metal bucket of water toward her. She tried again to kick, but her efforts were futile. The guard placed the bucket under her. The guards who were holding her set her down. She screamed as a flash of voltage raced through her body.

The Sun Storms had begun four hundred years earlier, destroying all electrical-based technology and explosive substances on the Earth. Half of the Ancients who lived at that time were either killed immediately or within the first year after the storms began. Four centuries later, the storms still raged against the Earth, forcing humans to ground their buildings and their footwear to prevent being electrocuted by the electrical ions in the air.

Two guards lifted Rebekah's feet out of the water. She took a deep breath, then they dropped her feet back into the water. She tried to endure the pain, but it wasn't like a cut or a burn. It was a pain that ravaged her entire body, and she could not help but scream. The guards pulled her feet out of the water again. Rebekah panted. Sweat was beading on her head. Rebekah could see all the prisoners watching from the cages lining the dirt road. Rebekah caught her uncle's eye and she could imagine his thoughts, 'Where is your God now?'

Rebekah didn't care what he or anybody else thought. This was for a purpose. She would endure it.

"Bring it on!" Rebekah spat at the guards.

The guards dropped her back into the water. They continued the process a few more times. One of the Saurian guards stood in front of Rebekah and grasped her face.

"Do you swear allegiance to her majesty, the glorious Queen?"

Rebekah's mind was beginning to be fuzzy. Her vision took a second to catch up to her eye movement. She was going through this for a reason. She had to be. It could not be all for nothing.

"Never," Rebekah said in slurred speech.

She was dropped back into the water. Rebekah could hear something. Off in the distance as she fell into the blackness. She recognized the sound. It was her screaming.

* * * *

REBEKAH COULD HEAR the morning horn blowing, but she couldn't open her eyes. She was so tired. Somebody pushed her. Somebody pushed her again. Rebekah forced herself to open her eyes. Della was sitting close to Rebekah, trying to wake her. Rebekah looked around. She was back in her cell. Most of the other prisoners were gone.

"You must wake. They will come for you soon," Della said. Della helped Rebekah up to a sitting position. "I am sorry. The Queen chose you because she thought you were my friend. She wants to hurt me by hurting you. The Dangarian Prince wished to harm you when you were brought in unconscious, but the other prisoners, Dangarian and Republic alike, stood to defy him."

"And my uncle?" Rebekah asked.

"Silently watched from the side."

Rebekah stood and brushed the dust from her clothes. She would show her uncle. There was a reason for the darkness she was in, and she only hoped she could be the light for him to see it.

"They come. Prepare yourself."

Rebekah looked. Four soldiers marched toward her cell. Two of the Saurian soldiers entered and dragged Rebekah out of the cell. She still was missing her grounding boots. The rocks in the road dug into her feet.

The guards led Rebekah to a female human servant dressed in white. The servant held a silver platter and ornamental cup filled with a clear liquid. The servant bowed and offered up the platter to Rebekah.

"Carry the tray without spilling the liquid," the servant announced.

Rebekah's heart sank. She thought she was being presented with a drink, but now it seemed that it was part of her *training*. Having been a waitress at her father's inn while in the Troit, it shouldn't be too hard of a task.

Rebekah took the platter from the servant. The cup was filled to the very top, and she accidentally spilled some of the liquid over the rim. A terrible pain shocked her in the back of the neck. She dropped the platter and fell to the ground. She looked up and saw one of the guards holding a thick metal rod.

"Carry the tray without spilling the liquid," the servant announced again.

Rebekah gathered up the tray and cup and stood up. The servant carefully filled the cup with water, stopping precisely at the rim. Rebekah stared at the cup. If she moved the platter even slightly, she would spill some of the liquid.

Rebekah took a deep breath, watched the cup, and took a careful step forward. Nothing spilled. She let out a sigh. She refocused and took another step, then another. Her bare foot landed on a rock. Her knee buckled and she tipped her cup over. The shock filled her head as the Saurian dug the rod into the back of her neck.

The rod was pulled away. The white that filled her vision cleared up and she could now see the dirt road. Rebekah panted for breath as she leaned on one knee and held the tray and the cup. She'd had enough. The platter and the cup was all she had, and they would have to do. Rebekah gripped the cup and quickly stood up, jamming the cup under the chin of one the soldiers. She side kicked the knee of the next closest guard. With the momentum from her kick,

Rebekah spun and grabbed her silver platter with both hands and struck a third Saurian guard in the neck. Her vision turned to pure white from the pain of the shocks against her head. She fell to the ground, but the shocks and the pain did not stop. Rebekah tried to stand, but a gloved fist struck her in the face, knocking her back to the ground. The shocks stopped. Rebekah laid on the ground, panting.

Her vision cleared up and Rebekah could see a Psi'Drakor standing above her. She could taste blood from an open cut in her mouth. Rebekah stood up and spit the blood into the Psi-Drakor's face.

The Psi-Drakor grabbed Rebekah by the throat and dragged her backwards, then slammed her back up against the same wooden pole that she had been tied to the night before. Her arms were cuffed behind her around the pole.

Rebekah saw another guard carrying the metal bucket of water towards her and she struggled to get free. The Psi-Drakor lifted her off the ground by her neck, then set her back down into the bucket of water. Rebekah screamed.

It felt like hours until Rebekah was lifted back out of the water. She didn't have time to catch her breath. The Psi-Drakor stepped forward and jammed a metal rod against her temple. Rebekah went blind, and she convulsed from the shock. The pain stopped. Before her vision cleared up, she felt herself being lifted and placed back into the water. They continued the process, over and over.

Rebekah's mind became cloudy. She couldn't concentrate. Where was she? Rebekah grasped for control, she would never give in. Who was she? She couldn't remember. The pain was unbearable. A word drifted in her mind. Rebekah. Yes, she was Rebekah. Rebekah grasped for something to hold her mind in place. She was losing control and drifting. The Saurians had done this, and they would pay. Rebekah grabbed ahold of one word in her mind. *Death.* They would all die. Every last one of them would die. Even if it had to be by her own hand. *Death.*

CHAPTER TEN
The Psi'Drakor

"It is not the critic who counts, not the man who points out how the strong man stumbled, or where the doer of deeds could have done better. The credit belongs to the man who is actually in the arena, whose face is marred by dust and sweat and blood, who strives valiantly, who errs and comes short again and again, who knows the great enthusiasms, the great devotions, and spends himself in a worthy cause, who at best knows achievement and who at the worst if he fails at least fails while daring greatly so that his place shall never be with those cold and timid souls who know neither victory nor defeat." - Theodore Roosevelt (1858 - 1919)

J AROD LEANED against the tree and watched the Special Forces soldiers laughing as they gathered around the campfire. They were on the outskirts of the new enemy border and it was the last night they would be allowed to have a campfire. Jarod had learned that it was typical for the Special Forces to spend that last night with laughter, good food, and warm thoughts. After that, their missions usually required long periods of silence, cold food, and cold nights.

Billy Thompson was the Special Forces rookie, so he was the brunt of many of their jokes. Jarod, on the other hand, had been accepted as part of the mission, but not necessarily as part of the team. His reputation preceded him, and the men were not sure how to deal with him, even though he was the youngest member of their team.

"You don't say much, do you?" Jordan said as he sat next to Jarod.

"I listen and watch. Talking is not my specialty."

"You say you are not a Paladin, but you read their literature," Jordan said, nodding at the book in

Jarod's lap.

"I actually know very little about the Paladins. I am anxious to speak with Paladin Markos when we return. Hopefully he will be able to answer many of my questions. Until then, I look for answers here," Jarod said, patting his book.

"Rest up. Your talents will be needed in the days ahead," Jordan said. He stood up and returned to the rest of the team.

* * * *

JORDAN LED the team through the forest that paralleled the major road leading south. The trees in the southern region still held their leaves, which provided cover.

Jarod followed Billy through the woods. Something was not right. There was a tingling and a high-pitched sound in the right side of his head. Eight tingling dots to be exact. Jarod could not explain it. He had never felt nor heard the sound before, but he knew there was something wrong.

Jarod quietly rushed passed Billy and the rest

of the team and took a place next to Jordan.

"What are you doing? Get back in place," Jordan said harshly.

"Jordan, I think there is something coming from the south," Jarod said, pointing in that direction.

Jordan raised a hand to halt the group. Each crouched behind a tree.

"Did you see something?"

Jarod shook his head. He was unable to explain the sense he had without sounding ridiculous.

"Hold for a minute is all I ask. You brought me because of my unique abilities. Just trust me on this one. There's something coming down the road. Eight of them."

Jordan looked at Jarod questioningly. Jordan shook his head, and then motioned to the team that eight enemies were coming from the south, and to hold their position.

Five minutes passed, but there was no activity from the road. Jarod could hear the men grumbling. Jordan looked over Jarod's shoulder at the men.

"Sorry Jarod, you must have been wrong," Jordan said. He motioned at the men to move out.

As quick as Jordan stood up, he sat back down. An arrow was protruding from his chest. More arrows flew through the trees around the men. The team quickly took cover behind the nearby trees. Jarod looked down the road and saw eight Saurian scouts standing there, preparing to fire again. He dove next to Jordan and steadied him against a large tree.

"You all right?"

"It punctured my lung," Jordan said. He was breathing hard.

Another barrage of arrows flew past the men and struck the trees nearby.

Jarod saw the Saurians running toward their positions to mount a ground assault.

Jarod motioned to Gilbert and Sven to cover Jordan. He motioned to the other four to follow him. It then occurred to him that he had just given orders. He had never been in a position to tell anybody what to do. He had always been bullied and told what to do by others. But he had given the orders without thinking, and the men obeyed.

Jarod took both swords in hand and raced out

of the trees toward the advancing lizard creatures. His initial thought was to take two, or possibly three, of the creatures. The other four men could get the rest. The creatures were in full stride. As he neared them, a weapons form like nothing he had ever envisioned entered his mind. It was so beautiful and fluid, but it was also the most lethal he had ever seen. He knew all twenty-five weapons forms, but this one surpassed all of them in both style and skill. All the other forms had been strike, pause, and block. This new form was one continuous motion where the subject performed a deadly dance of death with his partners.

As he neared the first Saurian, Jarod began the dance of the form. Jarod ducked the attack, slashed, and twirled, moving past the first Saurian and slashing at the next one. As he slashed with his right sword at the second Saurian, his left hand slashed backwards, slashing the backside of the first Saurian. The form did not include stabbing motions that would interrupt the dance. Instead, it used slashing techniques that had to be precise to hit vital unprotected body parts.

Jarod fought through the eight creatures, twirling and slashing, never once meeting sword to sword. He was gliding and dodging the Saurians' swings so that his dance would not be interrupted. He twirled passed the eighth creature and struck its backside. He turned to see a long line of dead Saurian bodies lying between him and his four team members. Billy's eyes were wide with fear. Perhaps he now realized how easily Jarod could retaliate against his bullying.

Jarod hated the killing and the death. It was easy to kill a rabbit or deer, but these Saurians were sentient beings. If they had tried a more political approach, Jarod would gladly have shared a dinner table with one of them. He had no real hatred or prejudice against them, but they were killing humans for the land. It was kill or be killed, and he chose not to be killed.

Jarod cleaned off the blood from his swords and returned to the rest of the team.

He motioned to the dead bodies, then to the nearby trees. "We need to hide the bodies. We do not want any other scouts to know we are in their lands," Jarod said,

"Yeah, but first, what…what was that? I have

never seen anything like it."

"That was the twenty-seventh weapons form, the *Dance of Death*."

"Are you saying there *are* more forms than the twenty-five?"

Jarod shook his head. "I believe there are five lost weapons forms, but I only know that one."

Michael looked at the dead bodies. He was the tallest of the Special Forces team, followed by Jarod himself. Michael stood eye to eye with Jarod, but he outweighed Jarod by twenty pounds.

"I am glad we never tangled that day in the army camp. I had my doubts about your abilities and your place on this mission, but it is now obvious that the rumors about you are actually true." Michael paused and looked at the dead bodies, then continued, "Can you save us a couple the next time, though?" he said with a smile as he slapped Jarod on the back.

Jarod smiled and blushed. "Sure."

After moving the bodies into the woods, the group surrounded Jordan. His breathing was labored, but steady.

"He needs to get back. I've stopped the bleeding, but the internal injuries are too great," Sven said.

Jordan labored as he spoke. "You go ahead, I can make it back."

Michael looked over at Sven, who then shook his head. "All right. We'll build a stretcher, and then Sven and Gilbert will carry the captain to the nearest doctor. The rest of us will go rescue the Princess. Let's move. We have wasted enough time."

After a half-hour, the team had crafted a stretcher that could be carried or hooked into harnesses strapped to the men's shoulders. Jarod had learned that the Special Forces were trained to create such "on the fly" devices. Their missions were usually far from cities – at least cities where they were welcomed.

Jarod watched the two men carry Jordan away. A part of him wished he could have been one of those men. He was sixteen. He had barely seen much of the world, yet here he was heading straight into enemy occupied territory with a group of five men. A year ago he would have thought the idea was ridiculous. Even now, the idea sounded pretty crazy. *Keep the faith*, Jarod told himself. It was what drove him forward and gave him courage to continue. He did not have much in the world, but it was the one thing he knew he could count on.

* * * *

JAROD LOOKED around the wall of the Saurian building. There was a row of ten cages lining the dirt road. Each cage held ten to twenty human prisoners. It had taken them a week to find the location. Nobody had dreamed they would have to seek out the princess and the king among so many prisoners. Jarod leaned against the wall of the building, along with the rest of the team.

"Can you sense them?" Michael asked.

Jarod nodded. "Like a hundred screaming dots in my head. If I knew which cage was hers, I could make it."

A female scream cut through the silent morning air. Michael surveyed the building with his looking glass, and then turned a shade whiter as he sat back down.

"We have a problem. That scream came from

the Princess. She's strapped to a pole in the middle of their courtyard. I also saw the King in the closest cells. He is the only one-armed man."

Michael handed Jarod the looking glass. "There is the King, and there, in the courtyard, is the Princess. Do you think you could open the first three cages, grab the King, and then return? I was hoping you might be able to tell where the Saurians are, and make it there and back undetected."

Jarod looked. A couple wooden buildings stood on the right side of the road leading up to the cells lining the left side of the road. Getting to the cells would not be a problem. He could sense where the Saurians were, and he knew which side of the building to hide behind. But the jail cells were out in the open, and although he knew where the creatures were, he could not tell if they were looking in his direction.

"Possibly. And the Princess?"

"Hopefully the distraction of running prisoners will allow us to free her."

Jarod nodded and closed his eyes. He used his sense to envision where the Saurians were stationed.

Most were around the courtyard or on the opposite side of the camp. As long as he stayed next to the roadside near the buildings, he should be all right. The prisoners would be able to see him, but most of them were watching the Princess in the square.

Jarod rounded the corner of the building and slowly began working his way toward the cells. There were only three buildings he had to use as cover, and he quickly rushed the gap between each one. He made it to the last building, then crouched down to peek around the corner into the square. The King's prison cell was only twenty feet to his left. Some of the prisoners had already spotted him, and they started making noises. He would have to hurry before they started drawing attention.

The Saurians were moving around too much. There was no way to know whether or not they were turning to see him. His only option was to release the prisoners as fast as he could and hope he didn't get shot by an arrow. He'd have to rely on the distraction to ensure a safe getaway with the King.

Jarod looked up the road. Something wasn't right. He could feel something rushing quickly toward him from down the road, but he could not see anything. He could not deny the feeling. It was starting to scream in his mind. Jarod looked down the road again. He could see puffs of dirt quickly rising into the air, as if somebody was running his way. Yet there was nothing in sight. Jarod ignored what he saw and trusted in the abilities he had been given. As he rolled forward he heard a thunderous chop strike the building where he had just been kneeling. He swung his sword backwards, hoping to hit something. He was startled when his swing was interrupted while on its way to hitting the building. He was even more surprised when he turned and saw that his sword had struck a Saurian right in its ribs. It wasn't dead. It took a swing at Jarod. Jarod ducked under the swing and spun around to pull his sword free. He stabbed backwards and drove the blade under the creature's armor and into its heart.

The battle had pulled Jarod away from the building and out into the open. All of the Saurians were now looking at him. Jarod ran for the King's cell, but he was forced to dive into a roll. He could sense the creatures surrounding him, but he could not see them. Jarod turned repeatedly, swinging his sword at each of the dots in his head, but all he heard was the sound of sword against sword.

Something tripped him up and sent him into the air. As he fell to the ground, he realized that one had slashed him with its tail. After he landed on the ground, an invisible fist struck him on the side of his face, and everything went black.

CHAPTER ELEVEN
Tricked

"We all live with the objective of being happy; our lives are all different and yet the same." - Anne Frank (1929 - 1945)

"I am a firm believer in the people. If given the truth, they can be depended upon to meet any national crises. The great point is to bring them the real facts." - Abraham Lincoln

DANIEL WAITED ALONE in the woods at the designated location. They had agreed to meet half way between Lansing and the supposed Saurian encampment. The meeting was to include Daniel, a Saurian leader, and a moderator. Daniel was not sure if the Saurians would keep their word, or if it was a trap. If they wanted him dead, there were easier ways than this. He considered the risk well worth it if it really meant freeing his daughter.

Nevertheless, the General was stationed with a squadron of men a mile north, in case Daniel did not return. If a Saurian leader showed up alone, Daniel could be sure that they had done the same.

A male Saurian approached with a sword in his hand. Daniel pulled out both of his swords. The Saurian was clothed differently than the others he had fought. The creature wore fine, ornamental armor fit for a general. The Saurian hissed at Daniel as they both circled and faced each other.

The sound of a female cough broke the tense silence, and both men looked toward the sound. Daniel recognized her as the one who had been communicating with him. The male Saurian's face showed his disgust as he looked at the moderator.

"Please drop your weapons where you stand and join me here," the female instructed.

Both men studied each other for a brief second, then they complied. Daniel smiled as he noticed the Saurian doing the same thing Daniel had done, spear his sword into the ground instead of just dropping it. This left the sword's hilt at waist height and easily retrievable if necessary.

Both men kept a distance of five feet between themselves as they walked closer to the female Saurian.

"I am glad to see that you both have accepted the terms for this meeting. I will be your moderator. I am hated by both sides, even though I work to help them both. Izikar'Etra, let me introduce Prince Daniel Lancaster, current ruler of the country Rembelshem. Prince Daniel Lancaster, let me introduce Izikar'Etra Sandamung'So, the Arc'Reisheen of the Saurian army.

Both men looked at each other, but did not say a word. The female Saurian walked closer to the two men.

"Hands up so I can check for weapons."

Reluctantly, both men lifted their arms as the moderator circled and patted them for hidden weapons.

Allowing the Saurian to touch him was the worst thing he could imagine, and it sent chills through his body; but for his daughter, he allowed it. He had no choice. That foolish kid Jarod was jeopardizing the Special Forces team's mission of saving his daughter, which meant Daniel had to free his daughter another way. The anger rose inside Daniel. If Jarod made it back alive…

The creature ran a hand down his arm. He forced the images of death out of his mind. He did not need a weapon to kill either of them. He restrained himself for one purpose, even if working against his instinct was the hardest thing to do. There was a sudden *clank* of metal, and the moderator jumped back away from the two men.

"What have you done, traitor!" the Saurian General yelled, grabbing at his arm.

A metal device was hooked on Daniel's right wrist and Izikar's left wrist. Daniel grabbed at his own wrist. The device was like the pre-storm handcuffs, but with a thick, two-foot metal bar holding the two men together instead of chains. Izikar reached for the moderator, which forced Daniel's arm to follow.

The moderator flapped its arms and quickly drifted ten feet backwards. Daniel wasn't sure what to be more shocked about; the creature's ability to fly or that he was chained up to one.

"Arc'Reisheen and Prince Daniel, there is only one way to get the ar'mkar removed, and it will take a considerable journey together to do so. I suggest you hurry. I have alerted the Saurian Queen and the Rembelshem Counselors that traitors were meeting at this location. They both have forces arriving soon. Although it would be interesting to see what each side would do with the both of you, it is in both our species' best interest that you survive, and maybe even learn to tolerate each other." The moderator then turned and ran back into the woods.

Izikar pulled and shook the device as he made noises that Daniel could only assume were from frustration.

"Come, filth. We have a long journey ahead and we need to remove ourselves from this location,"

Izikar said.

"Where do we have to go?"

Daniel saw the hatred in its eyes as the creature looked back at him.

"Back to the Saurian dwellings deep within the Earth."

CHAPTER TWELVE
The Coup

"Try not to become a man of success but rather try to become a man of value."
 - Albert Einstein (1879 - 1955)

"Love not the world, neither the things that are in the world. If any man love the world, the love of the Father is not in him." - I John 2:15

C OUNSELOR HADICAN stood and leaned against the wooden table. "Counselors, thank you for meeting under such precarious circumstances. But as you know, we seem to get disturbed more often than not."

Many of the counselors nodded and grumbled as they sat around the large, old wooden table. They had arrived sporadically during the day at a southern business district inn.

"You all know why this meeting was called. We must deal with the Lancaster family and remove them from the throne. The time to do it is now. King Robert and the Princess are missing or captive, and Prince Daniel has gone missing as well. It seems normal for the Lancaster family to turn up missing when their duties lie here."

"And what do you propose, Gerald? That you become the next King?"

"No, Counselor Landorf. I think the government could easily be run by the seven of us. Majority rules on issues. Four votes wins."

The counselors nodded and began talking amongst themselves.

"We all agree, then. Prepare your men. Tomorrow we take control of Rembelshem."

CHAPTER THIRTEEN
The Council of Greed

"Greedy eaters dig their graves with their teeth." - French Proverb

"A sound heart is the life of the flesh: but envy the rottenness of the bones."
- Proverbs 14:30

COUNSELOR HADICAN lifted his glass. "A toast." He waited as the other six counselors lifted their glasses. "To our perfect takeover of Rembelshem. Not a drop of blood lost and no citizen the wiser."

"Here, here," the counselors said, and then they sat back down at their table.

"Let us deal with our first issue. We need to remove all possible Lancaster loyalists from the palace," Counselor Hadican proposed.

"We have a war at hand and you are worried about a handful of staff?" Council Member Landorf responded.

"All are connected, Counselor Landorf. We have already achieved a great victory. In due time we will destroy the rest of these creatures. We have the greatest army in the lands. None can compare."

"A premature victory, do you not think? There are rumors of an army massing in the southern Republic as we speak. Rumors about giant lizard monsters twice the size of elephants."

Council Member Hadican was amused. "Giant lizard monsters? Now really, Counselor, shall we leave a candle burning in your bed chambers at night so you are not scared of the ghosts as well?" The room filled with laughter. "Our first priority is to get the General and the King's Guard out of the palace. To please Council Member Landorf, we will instruct them to take the army to defeat this *monster* army that is forming. It should be a swift battle, and we can eliminate this threat once and for all. Next, I suggest we remove any palace staff or persons occupying the castle. I tried to see the doctor today, but I was refused because the doctor was busy with two Sisters and some sniveling brat. Resources are being wasted needlessly. The doctor should only be available for Council Members and family."

"We have a war that could mean the end of our country and you are worried about not being able to see a doctor? That child is seriously sick and needs proper attention."

"Your war will be dealt with. All in favor of sending the army to finally squash these creatures? Unanimous. See, Counselor Landorf, we all share your goals. All in favor of removing unnecessary citizens from the palace? Six to one. Sorry, Counselor Landorf, majority rules. The Sisters and the brat will be re-moved from the palace. Okay, next topic. I propose that our next vote be to increase our wages…"

CHAPTER FOURTEEN
Freedom

"Is life so dear or peace so sweet as to be purchased at the price of chains and slavery? Forbid it, Almighty God! I know not what course others may take, but as for me, give me liberty, or give me death!"

- Patrick Henry (1736 - 1799)

MARKOS WAS IN PAIN as he awoke. His throbbing ankle felt like it was twice its normal size. He looked around. He had made camp at the site where the dragon had landed the night before. A new log had been put on the fire, and it blazed warmly. Markos looked around for the dragon, but it was nowhere to be seen.

"Hello?"

I am here, human.

The dragon suddenly became visible. It was laying twenty feet away. The sight of the dragon was disconcerting to Markos.

You are still in pain. Can you not heal yourself?

"No. I cannot use my gifts on myself. I would need another Paladin gifted in healing. Only few have such a talent and all the Paladins are currently in the field. I will just have to heal with time."

It does not make sense. If you can heal another, why can you not heal yourself?

Markos leaned down and picked up a piece of wood. "Like this piece of wood, I cannot pick myself off the ground. It is the same way with gifts. I can pick another person off the ground, the same I can also use my gifts on another person."

That is very interesting and gives me much to think about. I must know. How did you come across the dragon skin? I did not think it was possible for the skin of a dragon to survive after one's death.

"I do not know where it came from. It was my father's and where he got it I do not know."

The dragon walked closer to Markos and sniffed him. Markos swallowed. It took every ounce of will to stay still. When a head the size of half his body is sniffing you, it is hard not to picture being bitten.

The skin is of my genetic lineage by the color and the smell. And it keeps the same qualities as my skin has now? Resistance to heat and electricity? Amazing. Yes, you are confused. You see, the dragons can only survive on the Earth when the sun storms are active and there is enough ionization in the atmosphere. When a dragon dies, the electrical bonds of his skin and body dissipate and they exist no more. That is why there is no skeleton bones or carcasses to be found.

"Then how?"

I do not know. More I must think about. When

you are ready we will go and find your niece, I believe that is how you refer to her. I should be able to track her by using your genetics. She is made of similar genetic sequence as you, correct?

"Ah, if you mean, we share similar ancestors, then yes. My sister was her mother. You can track somebody by that?"

Yes. There is a different smell each one has. I should be able to find and follow her scent.

"Amazing. Before I ride again, if you will allow, I would like to make a saddle to help hold me on your back."

You have worries of falling?

Markos chuckled. "Considerable worries."

* * * *

REBEKAH WATCHED the Special Forces member be dragged across the courtyard by the Psi'Drakor. She was surprised, as were the Saurians, when he had killed the first Psi'Drakor, and even more surprised that he had briefly held three of them off. She knew why the Saurians had kept him alive. For the same reason she wanted him to stay alive – to find out how he had achieved such a feat. Rebekah tried to see who the man was as he was dragged by. She was shocked to see that it was just a boy. He looked familiar, but she could not place him. She must have seen him in the palace somewhere. The Psi'Drakor dragged the boy in front of their leader, and then a bucket of water was splashed over his head.

* * * *

JAROD WOKE ABRUPTLY and gasped for air as water washed over him. He was on his knees and being held up by two of the Saurians that looked like the invisible kind.

"Where are the others?" said the Saurian who was standing in front of Jarod.

"I am alone," Jarod said.

One of the soldiers slapped him across the face.

"Humans do not travel alone. We will find the others. Now, how did you protect yourself from the Psi'Drakor?"

Jarod figured that that must be the name of the invisible Saurians. He was not really sure what to tell the Saurian, so he decided to tell them the truth.

"By trusting in God."

The Saurian punched him in the face again. Jarod could taste the blood trickle down his mouth.

The leader turned to a female Saurian standing beside him. "Scan him and see how he does anything special." The Saurian male turned back to Jarod. "You will show us your tricks, or die. It is your choice." Then he nodded to the Psi'Drakor.

The Saurians let go of Jarod's arms and disappeared. Jarod could still sense their presence in his head. There were now five of them encircling him. A dot in Jarod's head came hurling toward him, and he was knocked to the ground by the Saurians invisible fist. Another dot came at him while he was on his hands and knees. He anticipated a kick, so he blocked his stomach. His arms were jarred as he was kicked. Jarod grabbed the invisible leg and swept with his own leg, catching the Saurians other leg and knocking it to the ground.

Another dot rushed in from behind. Jarod jumped into the air and did a spinning side kick. His timing was slightly off, but he still caught the Saurian in the chest or head and he felt it fall backwards to the ground.

The five dots in his head were circling him more quickly now. Three of them swarmed him. Jarod blocked a punch and a kick, but the third kicked him from behind, sending him to the ground. Jarod tried to spit the dirt from his mouth as he stood up, but a tail whipped around and knocked his legs out from under him, sending him into the air. He landed on his back.

The kicks came quickly, and he could not block them all. A hard kick sent him twirling across the ground and against the Princess's legs and pole. The princess yelled in pain.

Pain shot through his side. He knew he had broken a couple of ribs.

"I am sorry, Princess," Jarod said, breathing into the dirt.

"I am fine, sir. Stay down, they may spare you."

"Not until you are free."

Invisible arms grabbed him again and dragged him in front of the leader.

"Anything?" he asked the female next to him. She shook her head. "For a human, you are trained well, and I am sure you will take your secret to your death. But, what about the death of your Princess? Are you willing to sacrifice her life to keep your secrets?"

The princess screamed in agony. Jarod turned his head and saw the two Saurians putting her back into more water. Jarod struggled to stand up as the arms held him firmly against the ground. The screams stopped as the princess was lifted from the water.

"What is your secret, human?"

Jarod's vision flashed. He thought he might be passing out. All the color of the world was slowly turning dark. But it wasn't total darkness, and he was still awake. White and gray dots filled the blackness outlining the Saurian leader, the trees, the rocks, the houses, and the invisible Saurians. He was seeing the world at a different level, almost down to the basic building blocks of molecules.

His hands grew warmer and began to tingle as streams of white ions raced from the air, forming a solid object within his hands. They continued in both hands, growing rapidly outward until he could see that he was holding two blazing swords of electrical fire.

The invisible Saurians let go of Jarod's arms and drew their weapons as they jumped away from him. Jarod stood up and looked around. The Saurian leader, along with the multitudes of Saurians, gasped as they stepped back away from Jarod. One of the Psi'Drakor rushed at Jarod. Jarod spun away from the Psi'Drakor's swing, then swung at him with his sword. Jarod never felt any contact. The tip of his sword struck the ground. The Saurian made a hissing sound as it fell to the ground in two halves.

He did not have long to think about what had just happened as more Psi'Drakors rushed at him. Jarod launched himself into the Dance of Death. He could not strike sword against sword, so it was the best form to use. He dodged the swings, spun around, and repeatedly slashed the front and backsides of his attackers. In moments, ten Psi'Drakor lay in pieces in an encompassing circle where Jarod had been held.

Jarod turned toward the princess. The two guards holding her turned and ran in opposite directions.

* * * *

REBEKAH GASPED. Within seconds she had

watched the Special Forces member produce swords of fire like the one she had once held, and then dispatch a multitude of invisible Psi'Drakors. The officer had twisted, turned, and struck at what looked to be just air. But pieces and bodies of Saurian soldiers had appeared out of thin air and fell to the ground.

But what had surprised her most was when he had turned toward her. It was his eyes, or the absence of his eyes, as bright light streamed from the sockets. Then he began to walk toward her. She wasn't sure whether to be afraid or thankful. Her thoughts about the Special Forces soldier vanished as she heard a roar from the skies.

*****

JAROD SLICED the bonds from the princess, and then turned suddenly as he heard a rumbling roar coming from the sky. The swords of fire disappeared from his hands and the colors of the world returned in a snap, causing Jarod to stumble from the nauseating effect.

A Saurian crowd was still gathered after witnessing Jarod's display against the Psi'Drakor. The dragon swooped down and breathed a blast of fire through them. Jarod flung himself over the princess to protect her from the blast. The heat pounded against his back. Once the dragon's blast subsided, Jarod released the princess. He grabbed two of the Psi'Drakor swords and placed himself into a defensive position between the princess and the dragon and the Saurians. Jarod was not sure what the tiny swords would do against a fire-breathing dragon, but the dragon was far from being as powerful as God, so Jarod was not afraid.

Jarod glanced back quickly, then turned back to the dragon. "Are you alright, Princess?" Jarod asked. He had not been able to get a good look at the princess, but something about her seemed familiar.

The dragon turned in the air and began to fly back in their direction. Jarod gripped his swords tighter and continued to keep his body between the dragon and the princess. The dragon gracefully landed near them and Jarod was astonished to see a man slide off the dragon's back.

"Markos!" the princess yelled. She ran past Jarod to give the big man a hug.

Paladin Markos?

"Jarod!"

Jarod turned toward the sound of the call to find Michael and the other Special Forces opening the cells to free the prisoners. He looked around for the princess. She was talking to the rider of the dragon. If it was Paladin Markos, Jarod wanted desperately to talk to him. But this was not the time. The man helped the princess onto the back of the dragon, then he grabbed a strap and climbed on himself. There really was not much more Jarod could do if the princess was being protected by Paladin Markos and a fire-breathing dragon. Jarod turned and ran to help the rest of his team.

* * * *

"MARKOS, are you sure about this?" Rebekah asked.

Markos climbed onto the dragon and sat behind Rebekah. "I would not put my only niece in harm's way."

"Niece?"

"That's right. You don't know. A lot has transpired since you have been gone. I have much to tell on our journey home," Markos said with a smile.

"What about the King and the Special Forces Officer?" Rebekah said as she turned and saw the man running toward the prisoners.

"It looks like there are more Special Forces to help out now," Markos said, pausing to look at the scattered remains of the Psi'Drakor. "And from that mess, it looks like he doesn't need my help at the moment. Although, I will definitely be talking to him later."

"Everything happened so quickly and I never got to see or meet him. You know who he is then? He looked like just a boy."

"Based on your description and on the man calling his name, I can only assume that he is Jarod the Great."

CHAPTER FIFTEEN
Freedom Lost

"Guard with jealous attention the public liberty. Suspect everyone who approaches that jewel. Unfortunately, nothing will preserve it but downright force. Whenever you give up that force, you are ruined."

- Patrick Henry (1736 - 1799)

R EBEKAH LOOKED at Markos in shock and confusion. "What?!" Rebekah exclaimed. *"Uncle Markos* was just a name that Thad and I called you. You can't be my real uncle!"

"I assure you, Rebekah, you are my real niece. Hannah, your mother, was my sister. Remember when I talked about my sister playing the violin, and you said your father learned to play the violin because of your mother? I know your father well, or at least I thought I did. He is no longer the man he once was. He was wounded during the battle to break the siege, but he is doing well now."

"He was hurt?!"

"Yes, badly in fact. He took an arrow in the chest and a spear in his side. He has healed fine. When I left, he had just put the King's Council in their place. It sounds like you had done the same," Markos said with a smile.

Rebekah smiled and blushed. "Yes, they are an untrustworthy lot. But back to more important matters, Uncle Markos. Out of all the people I could have met to travel with, it was you? Absolutely amazing."

Markos smiled knowingly. "Yes. I believe you will begin to see many unexplainable events happening more often."

They had traveled a good portion of a day, until they were out of the Saurian occupied territory. Then they landed so Markos could check on Rebekah's health and get food and drink. Markos had Sjvek land next to an abandoned farmhouse.

Rebekah moved closer to Markos and whispered, "Ok, what is up with you riding a dragon?"

I am still here human; you do not need to whisper.

"Whoa! It talks?"

Markos smiled. "Uncanny isn't it. They are actually very intelligent, more so than even the Saurians. Do you remember my story about my father finding the men destroying all the eggs but one? Meet Sjvek. He is the one that hatched."

"But that would mean his mother…"

"Was the dragon that killed my parents. Your grandparents. Dragons are actually forbidden to kill humans, and he will question his mother when he returns home."

"Have you had enough food?" Markos asked, offering a piece of bread.

"Yes, thank you."

"After what you have been through, I'm thankful that I cannot see any internal damage. A few days of pampering from the palace servants and you will be back to normal."

"Ha, ha, ha," Rebekah said sarcastically. "That is the hardest thing to get used to. I have served others all my life, and when I am at the palace I have five maids fussing over me. "

"Sjvek, are you able to carry us further without any problems?"

Easily enough. I will need to drop you off a distance from the city. I have already broken a considerable number of laws as it is.

"I understand, and I thank you for all you have done. A couple more days and I am afraid my niece would have no longer been with us." Markos looked at Rebekah. "Let's get going. Your father has gone through a lot to get back to you. He will be relieved to finally have you back."

* * * *

"HERE, WEAR my cloak," Markos said as he handed Rebekah his black cloak.

"Thank you," Rebekah said as she pulled the cloak around her shoulders. "I love this time of year. I could spend hours just staring at the hills full of orange and red leaves.

"I prefer Spring myself. Autumn is a reminder that snow is on its way, and Duke and I have had our share of close calls in some snowstorms as we've traveled. No, give me the smell of the first Spring rain and the multitudes of flowers any day."

Rebekah continued to admire the orange and red leaves that filled the surrounding hills as they slowly rode Duke back to Lansing. Sjvek had dropped them off at the abandoned Paladin Complex located several miles west of Lansing, then they removed his saddle and he flew away. Markos had found Duke in his stall, just where he'd hoped. Markos said it was the first time he had ever had to send Duke away from combat, and it was a relief to see that the training had paid off.

They crested the same hill that they had walked together many months ago. Rebekah had been waiting for a glimpse of the capital city. After being taken captive and tortured, she longed for the security of the palace walls. Rebekah's thoughts turned dark. The walls had not prevented her from being taken prisoner. She did not know which counselor had helped in her capture, but she knew his voice. If necessary, by a dagger's edge, she would make each one talk.

"You must be getting excited. It has been awhile since you have seen your father," Markos said.

"Yes, so much has happened, and there's so much to talk about. But once the hugging is done, he is in trouble. He has a lot of explaining to do. Me being the Princess of Rembelshem? Him a Weapons Master? Yeah, a lot of explaining to do."

Markos chuckled. "Glad I am not him."

Markos and Rebekah followed a line of people across the large wooden bridge that covered the deep defensive ditch. The line moved slowly until they reached the front and were directed to one of the guards at a table.

"Name, where are you from, where are you going, and for how long?"

Markos reached inside his tunic and showed the man a medallion hooked to a chain necklace. "Paladin Markos Axebearer," was all Markos said.

"Paladin Markos, it is an honor." The guard looked at Rebekah. "Princess Lancaster?" The man stood quickly from his seat and bowed. "Wait here, I will have an escort prepared."

"That is alright, I can see the Princess to the palace."

"No, I insist. It is our duty to protect the Princess. If I were to let her go alone and something were to happen, I would be imprisoned for life. Please, just a minute."

The man ran through a door leading into the exterior wall, and within minutes a dozen guards had surrounded Rebekah.

"I don't miss this part," Rebekah whispered to Markos.

Markos smiled reassuringly. "It looks like you are in capable hands. Hopefully the Paladin leaders have returned. I have to inform them about my findings with the…" Markos paused, "with Sjvek and his family."

"Good luck. That should be an interesting conversation. I will miss hearing you tell them of your recent high-altitude riding excursions."

Markos laughed. "Very true. Well, I will see you soon." He gave Rebekah a hug.

Rebekah waved as the guards began moving forward, leaving Markos standing at the gate. Rebekah turned and looked ahead. Now it was time to see her father again. So much had happened in the six months since she had last seen him. She could barely remember the simple, small-town innkeeper's daughter she had once been.

Rebekah followed as the guards created a path through the busy streets of the business district, up through a residential district, and finally up the stairs to the royal level. The palace loomed ahead, and it looked beautiful and comforting in the afternoon light and blue sky.

The guards paused as they entered the palace. The lead officer spoke briefly with a palace guard. The officer then resumed his position and led the group up the western section. Rebekah thought this was odd, since her living quarters were in the eastern section of the palace. She assumed that her father must be in the western section for some reason.

The lead guard led them to a door, knocked, and then entered. He returned, and then motioned the guards into the room. Rebekah's heart was pounding. What would she say first?

Rebekah stepped through the doorway and looked around the study for her father, but she did not see him. There were only two older men standing by a desk. Rebekah recognized them instantly. They were two of the King's counselors.

Rebekah reached for her sword, but she didn't have one. "What is going on?" Rebekah demanded.

One of the men stepped away from the desk and walked toward her. "Princess, it is such a relief to know you are alive. We feared the worst when we heard you had been taken captive by the creatures. It is quite a surprise, actually. An unwelcome surprise, unfortunately. We did not think we would need to deal with you. With King Robert and you taken captive and your father missing, the counselors had no choice but to take over the Rembelshem governing powers from the Lancaster family."

"You had no choice? Where is my father?!"

"We really do not know. Your father left the palace of his own accord and nobody has seen him since. But for now, you have created a problem that we did not expect. Take her to the jail cells."

The other council member stepped forward. "The jail cells? She should at least be confined to her living quarters. She is still the Princess."

"Until we figure out what to do with her, she needs to be confined in secrecy. We cannot afford another uprising." The counselor looked back to the lead guard. "Your team is released of its previous duties, and it must now guard the Princess until further notice. Keep the knowledge of her existence quiet, or else you will be guilty of treason. Make sure she is fed and well cared for. If any harm comes to her, all of you will pay dearly. Who else knows that she is inside the city?"

"Paladin Markos brought her, Sir."

"Of all the people, it would be him. I'll take care of it."

"She is his niece; he will not be quiet," the other counselor retorted.

"He has no choice. He will be forced to sever the Paladin and Rembelshem agreement if he meddles in affairs of the state."

"Go."

"Wait," Rebekah pleaded. "When I was captured by the Saurians, one of the counselors was involved. He is working with the Saurians to overthrow the humans."

"Ridiculous. None of us would stoop that low. Take her away."

Rebekah had no choice but to follow the guards. She was unarmed and outnumbered. She wanted to scream. She could not believe that she was a prisoner once again. She had been a prisoner of her uncle the King, the Saurians, and now the King's Council. She hoped there was a reason.

One good thing had come from the meeting with the counselors. She could cross two of the counselors off her list. Neither had the voice of the traitor. Perhaps she had also planted a seed of doubt within the counselors that would later prove fruitful.

CHAPTER SIXTEEN
His will

"For everything there is a season,
And a time for every matter under heaven:
A time to be born, and a time to die."
- Ecclesiastes 3:1-2

"Thy kingdom come, Thy will be done in earth, as it is in heaven."
- Matthew 6:10

SISTER ELIZABETH PATTED Thadius's head with the damp cloth. Since being removed from the Royal Palace she had no access to a doctor or any fever reducing medicines. While staying at the palace they had been able to keep the young boy's fever under control, but now without the medications, the fever was constant.

After being escorted from the palace, Sister Elizabeth and Sister Abigael returned to the Lansing-based Paladin complex with Thadius. The first day at the complex, the child had improved and the Sisters thought the worst of the illness was finally over. The days that followed showed they had been wrong.

The Sister dipped the cloth back in the bowl of water on the table nearby. She squeezed the cool water from the cloth and laid it back on Thadius's head. The door opened to the small cottage and Sister's Elizabeth's heart raced for good news.

Sister Abigael entered the cottage and shook her head.

Sister Elizabeth's heart dropped. All the Paladin's gifted in healing were gone on missions and the fever reducing medicines that would help Thadius had not yet been restocked after the siege. Only the King's personal doctor had access to supplies within the palace, but they no longer had access to his help. Sister Abigael had been out searching the city again to see if the medicines had been delivered to any of the city doctors. From Sister Abigael's gloomy look, she knew none had.

Thadius opened his eyes, but they fluttered from the strength it took to keep them open. He smiled when he caught sight of the sisters. He tried to lift himself from the bed but his arms wobbled from the lack of strength to do so.

"Shhhh… stay still Thadius. Just close your eyes and rest."

Thadius did as instructed and he seemed to relax at the sound of Sister Elizabeth's voice. Sister Elizabeth's eyes flowed with tears once again as she helplessly watched the shivering boy.

"How is it that everything seems to be working against this young child?. It just doesn't make sense," Sister Elizabeth stated.

Sister Abigael laid a hand on her shoulders. "I cannot even begin to fathom God's master plan and how this child is involved in it. I hope one day I will know because this is the hardest trial of faith I have ever gone through. His will be done."

"His will be done," Sister Elizabeth said in acknowledgement. "How long do you think he has?"

Sister Abigael looked at the boy and sighed. "At this rate, I would say he might have a day or two."

CHAPTER SEVENTEEN
A New Path

"The moral and religious system which Jesus Christ transmitted to us is the best the world has ever seen, or can see."

– Benjamin Franklin (1706 - 1790)

J AROD THOUGHT of Thadius and smiled. He could not wait to get back and see the little rug rat. Then he would probably head home to find his family, if they were alive.

"Now listen here, peasant scum. I am the Prince of Dangaria, and I will be treated as such!"

Jarod looked behind him and saw an older teenage boy yelling at Billy. Jarod shook his head. The King had insisted that all the prisoners, not just him, would be escorted and under the protection of the five Special Forces members. Jarod was convinced that he would rather go into battle against the Saurians any day than babysit a hundred whiney and self-centered dignitaries from three different countries.

Each of the five Special Forces members were positioned around the group for protection. Jarod walked a small distance from the section of freed prisoners to which he had been assigned. Everybody had witnessed his display against the invisible Saurians, and most of the former prisoners moved away from him if he got too close. The four Special Forces members did not shy away from him, but they were obviously uneasy about being close to him.

Jarod slowed his pace. The group around Billy was getting louder and more aggressive. Suddenly, the alarms in Jarod's mind starting going off. Jarod quickly put a hand over the loud Dangarian Prince's mouth, shoved him against a tree, and then held him in place. Jarod closed his eyes to concentrate on the dots in his mind. He felt the power begin to flow through his body, and then he opened his eyes. He heard the gasps from all those around him. The prince he was holding fainted. Jarod let go and the prince fell limp to the ground.

Jarod spoke in the direction where he had last remembered seeing the leader. "Michael. Ten Saurians. Invisible. South." In this state he could not tell who was who.

"How far?" Michael asked from a distance.

Jarod closed his eyes to concentrate. "Maybe two minutes."

"Men take positions around the group. Jarod protect the King."

Billy spoke up. "But, they are invisible, sir. Jarod, what do we do?"

But Jarod did not get a chance to answer.

"Soldiers of Rembelshem, hear me now," yelled a man's voice beside Jarod. "For centuries, I and my forefathers have tried to abolish religion from the Rembelshem lands. On this day, I will tell you I have been wrong. There is no way to squash what is greater than us. You cannot live through the faith of another man, but on this day, you must find your own. Drop the sins and cares of this world and let God be on your side. Believe and you will see. Do not believe, and you will surely die."

"Care to lend one of your swords, young man?" King Robert asked.

"I…uh…yes, sir. I mean, Your Majesty," Jarod stammered, handing one of his swords to the man standing beside him.

Jarod was caught off guard by the King's request. The King of Rembelshem had just implored his men to believe and follow God. Jarod focused back on the Saurians. He was tasked with protecting the King and he had guaranteed that the King would not need to use the sword.

"Thirty seconds!" Jarod yelled.

Whimpering grew louder in the central circle

of country leaders and dignitaries. Jarod slid his other sword into his back sheath. He would not need it. Jarod looked at his hands and focused as he called forth the swords of fire. He watched as white particles streamed from the electrically charged air and filled his hands. Jarod flexed his hands, feeling the strange sensation of having a solid object in his hands. The particles continued to be drawn from the surroundings and then tapered away once Jarod held two blazing white swords of electrical fire.

"Get behind me, Your Majesty."

"But…"

Jarod could see the forms of the Saurians running toward the group.

"Get behind me, now!"

"I see them!"

"I see them, too. Get ready men, here they come."

The Saurian group split apart. Five joined a group and ran toward Jarod while the other five separated and advanced toward the other Special Forces members. Metal against metal rang from the opposite side of the circle. Jarod could not tell what was happening. The group of five Psi'Drakor paused cautiously in front of Jarod. Jarod took a defensive stance in front of the King and held up the blindingly bright swords. The Psi'Drakor hesitated, and then Billy and Michael attacked the group from opposite sides. The middle three Saurians rushed toward Jarod.

Jarod had been charged with protecting the King and he would not allow the Saurians to get close. Jarod raised the two swords over his head and threw them at the advancing Psi'Drakor. The flaming swords ripped through two of the attackers and dissipated upon exiting their backs. Jarod grabbed the metal sword from his back scabbard and threw it as he had done the others, striking the last Saurian in the chest and sending it to the ground.

"Clear!"

"Clear!"

"Clear!"

The Special Forces members yelled out their status around the circle. Jarod's vision returned to normal and he looked around. His team members were busily retrieving and cleaning daggers and swords from the dead Saurians, while the mass of people they were protecting began to stand up from their huddled positions. Jarod retrieved his own sword, and after cleaning it, returned it to its scabbard. Jarod looked at the King, who was still holding his sword. He offered it back to Jarod.

"Thank you," Jarod said.

"Thank you. I could have managed to put up a defense, but I was never trained to rely on fighting with my left hand alone."

"No, I mean, thank you for your speech. It was unexpected, but needed. I am confused about what has changed your views."

"Nothing in particular…but many things. You, for example. Even without the," the king paused and motioned to Jarod's hand and eyes, "swords and eye business, people can tell there is something different about you. Then there is the Princess. She has shown that she is willing to die not only for her belief in the human race but for her belief in her God. For centuries people have tried to bring peace to our three nations, and in one week her beliefs have done just that. If she says she will protect these people, they know she means every word of it. They will follow her for it, as would I. That achievement is beyond anything a human could ever do on his own."

Jarod nodded. He understood, and he was amazed that the king understood so clearly as well.

Billy approached. "Your Majesty," he said with a bow. "Jarod, Michael wants to know if you sense anything."

Jarod shook his head. "We are clear for now."

"Michael, we are clear to move!"

Michael shouted orders to his men from the other side of the circle.

Billy began to walk away, hesitated, and then finally spoke to Jarod. "I…I don't understand. There are so many questions."

"There will be many more. You have chosen a path that is harder than any you have ever taken. You have discipline for your body, but discipline for your mind and soul will be harder yet." Jarod reached into his pack, retrieved his burgundy colored book, and then handed it to Billy. "You will begin to find your answers here."

Billy took the book and held it as if it were a fragile object. "I couldn't."

"It was given to me by a friend, just as I now give it to a friend."

"But…"

Jarod held out an arm and Billy clasped it in return. The one-time bully and coward locked arms and eyes as their grievances between each other disappeared.

The leader called Billy's name. "Thank you," Billy said, as he held up the book up and ran off toward Michael.

A hand was laid on Jarod's shoulder and the king stood next to him. "There is quite a story there isn't there?"

Jarod smiled. "Yes, Your Majesty. As you said, there are certain events that are beyond anything we could ever achieve on our own."

CHAPTER EIGHTEEN
Betrayed

"An individual who breaks a law that conscience tells him is unjust, and who willingly accepts the penalty of imprisonment in order to arouse the conscience of the community over its injustice, is in reality expressing the highest respect for the law." – Martin Luther King Jr. (1929 - 1968)

THE QUEEN STOOD outside her tent and analyzed the scene. The slave cages' doors were open and all the prisoners were gone. Her people were busily running around the square. Some were forced to clean the remnants of the destruction against the Psi'Drakor. Her people doing such menial labor! As much as she hated the thought of bringing more humans back into the camp, she would have to start the process of capturing more of the disgusting creatures as slaves.

Her people were confused by the day's events. She was confused by the day's events, but she could not appear alarmed to her people. From a distance, she had witnessed the massacre of the invisible Psi'Drakor by a human! A human who could see the Psi'Drakor and wield weapons of unimaginable power. The revelation was frightening. But more frightening was the fact that a human had tamed a dragon! She did not know which images would haunt her more; body parts of the invisible Psi'Drakor exploding into view or the dragon's fire turning multitudes of her people into ash.

What has happened?

The Queen was unprepared for the encounter with the voice in such an open location.

The human slaves have escaped is what has happened! The queen thought harshly.

Odd. But it does not matter anymore. The humans have begun to launch their attack, and their soldiers now march this way. Prepare...the final battle is at hand. You will soon have as many slaves as you wish.

The humans now wield weapons that are beyond our own. How shall we fight against that?

Only one or two humans possess such abilities. Do not be worried about them. They will be dealt with soon.

And what of the dragons?

What about the dragons?

A dragon ridden by a human reduced a number of Saurians to ashes with its fire!

What!? Impossible! The voice shouted in the Queen's mind, and then paused shortly before continuing. *Prepare your troops. The other matters will be dealt with.*

CHAPTER NINETEEN
The Plan Revealed

"*To put the world right in order, we must first put the nation in order; to put the nation in order, we must first put the family in order; to put the family in order, we must first cultivate our personal life; we must first set our hearts right.*" - Confucius

SJVEK PAUSED outside the cave entrance. It was a beautiful sunny day and he was not ready to enter the darkness of the cave. To be honest with himself, he was not yet ready to face his mother. How would he bring up what he had learned in a conversation?

"Good morning, mother. Oh, by the way, did you kill some humans a few decades ago?"

"Sjvek, why would you ask such a thing?"

"Well you see, I was breaking one of the High Laws myself and I was sitting around chatting with this human after I saved his life and..."

Needless to say, he knew that conversation would not end well.

Sjvek entered the cave mouth and descended into the dragon dwellings. He was a dragon and feared nothing, except for his mother. As the leader of the dragons, she ruled with strict adherence to what the dragons were allowed or disallowed to do. None dared oppose her will. It was not the dragon way. *None, that is, until her son had been compelled to save a human with whom he shared a strange bond,* Sjvek thought.

Sjvek followed the twists and turns of the passageways toward his and his mother's living spaces. Sjvek slowed. He could feel the presence of others. But worse, he felt strong vibrations from his mother. She was not happy. As he grew closer, he sensed that she was furious. Sjvek concentrated and searched with his mind to find the waves of communications. He could tell there were four dragons communicating with each other. He delicately folded his thoughts into the chat. One wrong thought and they would know what he had done.

We will use it to our benefit. The Saurian Queen believes the humans tamed a dragon. We will ensure that she keeps thinking we are dumb animals.

And what of this rogue dragon?

Find out who it was and bring him to me. We will need to deal with him secretly. If the others find out, questions will arise. Soon, the Humans and Saurians will begin their final battle against each other. As a unified force we will be able to rid the world of what is left of both sides.

Sjvek panicked and lost his concentration.

Who's there?!

Sjvek detached himself from the conversation

and rushed out of the corridor. He fled toward the general population living quarters. He needed to hide in the grouping of his fellow dragons. Sjvek slowed his pace and entered the closest community center cavern.

The large cavern was filled with dragonlings scurrying around and twenty dragons mingling in conversation. Sjvek could not exactly hide in the grouping, but he felt safer in a more public arrangement. Blue, green, black, and various other colored dragons filled the location, but Sjvek's coloring marked him as a descendant of the leaders. Only he and his mother were the last surviving dragons with the pink and purplish tone skin.

Sjvek drew himself into the game with the dragonlings. He was still a teenager in dragon years, and he did not have much in common with the adults yet. It was not uncommon for him to play with the dragonlings. If any came looking, it would appear normal.

The giant black dragon, Korj, burst into the community center. He was followed by the slightly smaller brown and green dragon accomplices, and finally by the elegant entrance of his mother.

His mother and three dragons approached the adults in conversation. After a brief moment, all heads turned Sjvek's way.

Go to your parents, little ones. Sjvek commanded the dragonlings.

His mother turned from the group, approached, and spoke to him alone. *Sjvek, you have broken one of our commandments and now you see why it is so vital to obey. You only heard part of the conversation and do not understand the full scope of what is being said.*

His mother paused a short distance away and sniffed the air. Fear engulfed Sjvek as he watched his mother's eyes turn to hatred. *It was you! The stench of the human still lingers on your skin. What were you thinking? Do you know what you have done?*

Sjvek's mother's anger burst forth toward him as flames. Sjvek instinctively protected himself by pulling the ions from the air into a wall before him. Flames burst upward and around the invisible barrier.

What is this?!

Sjvek opened his conversation to all who could

hear in the dragon dwellings. *There is more to this world than you even know Mother. There is one far greater than you.*

Ekra roared in anger and threw her body into her son, smashing him into the stone wall.

You have chosen a path to destroy the Humans and Saurians because of hatred. Three decades ago you killed humans for killing my brother and sisters. You killed the wrong humans! Let go of your hatred, Mother.

Ekra drew another breath to release more flames toward her son. Sjvek created a new invisible wall and willed it toward his mother. The wall caught her by surprise, lifting her into the air and throwing her backwards.

Sjvek raced passed the big black dragon guarding the door. He ran through the cave corridors and burst into the open sunlight flapping his wings to get away. He had just separated himself from his family…his kind. He was scared and did not know what to do. He needed help. He needed to find Markos.

* * * *

WHAT DO we do about him? Korj asked.

Ekra responded, *He has broken too many laws and has caused chaos among the dragons. There is only one thing to do. Kill him. Kill him and any human or Saurian that stands in your way. We do not need to hide anymore. The Earth will be ours soon enough.*

CHAPTER TWENTY
Death

"There is no pain so great as the memory of joy in present grief.."
- Aeschylus (525 BC - 456 BC)

"To everything there is a season, and a time to every purpose under the heaven." - Ecclesiastes 3:1

MARKOS RAN a finger across the young boy's name engraved on the tombstone. If only he had arrived sooner, maybe he could have healed him. If only...*His will be done.* Markos knew he could not understand the plan. He only had to trust in it. Sister Abigael and Sister Elizabeth stood on each side of him in the Paladin Complex cemetery. Markos gave Sister Elizabeth a reassuring hug as she began to cry.

"Paladin Markos, I am sorry to disturb you," said a man's voice.

Markos released Sister Elizabeth and turned toward the man. Jordan was accompanied by two other Special Forces members. None showed any signs of tension in their stance and Markos did not sense that any more were in hiding. Normally, a Special Forces team entering the Paladin compound without permission would violate their treaty with the Rembelshem government, so the circumstances must truly be serious for Jordan to enter without such permission. Not that Markos was worried. The Sisters were prepared for any battle. Both were dressed in their white armor and had their weapons. They were specially trained to fight in two's. Even he would have trouble trying to fight against two Sisters.

Markos turned to the tombstone one last time, and then exited the cemetery as the Sisters followed.

"Jordan, what brings you out here?"

"The Princess. She has been imprisoned by the King's Council."

Markos's heart ached. "I know."

Jordan looked confused. "You know and you have not done anything about it?"

"I cannot. Unfortunately, there is more at stake if I were to break the agreement between the Paladin and the Rembelshem government. Even though the Princess is my niece, I cannot do anything."

Jordan nodded.

"Do you have a plan?" Markos asked.

"I come seeking your guidance. I was hoping you would have talents to find Prince Daniel."

Markos shook his head. "The Paladins do not have such abilities. Has the other half of he Special Forces team arrived?"

"Not yet, but we expect them soon."

Markos?

Sjvek?

Yes, I need your help.

"What should we do then?" Jordan asked.

Markos raised a hand. "Once second, Jordan."

Where are you, Sjvek? What is wrong?

I am on the outskirts of your location. I have vital information about the Human and Saurian war, and now I am in danger.

"Markos, is everything alright?" Sister Elizabeth asked worriedly.

"Yes, one second, please," Markos replied.

How are you in danger? Is somebody there?

Not yet, but I fear I will be hunted soon.

There is a large open space outside this building. Meet me there.

"Come," Markos said as he hurried outside the mess hall. "Don't be afraid or attack. He is welcome here."

"Who?" Sister Abigael asked.

The dust from the complex square began to swirl, and it forced everybody to cover their eyes.

"Markos?" Sister Elizabeth asked.

Markos heard the sounds of swords being

drawn.

"Stand down now or I will personally remove the weapons from your hands," Markos yelled over the sound of the wind.

Suddenly the wind died down in the courtyard and everything seemed back to normal.

"Sjvek, you may show yourself."

The young red dragon materialized in the middle of the courtyard. The Sisters and Special Forces men gasped, but held their swords sheathed.

"Everybody, meet Sjvek. I can't explain now, but something is after him. I need everybody to take guard around him."

Markos walked up to the dragon and patted its side. The two Sisters and three Special Forces watched Markos in awe as they made a circle around the dragon.

What is wrong, Sjvek?

My mother is after me.

You are worried about your mother?

You don't understand. She knows I helped you. But worse, I found out she is behind the fights among the humans and Saurians. It is her goal for the humans and

Saurians to rid the world of each other. She will send other dragons to find me. I have put you in harm's way and I need to go, but you need to stop this war.

You are protected here. By us and by One greater than any your mother can send. To stop this war, I need your help. Remember my niece who you helped to save? Is it possible for you to track her from the other half of her genetic lineage as you tracked her from mine?

You mean to find her father?

Yes, exactly!

That should not be a problem.

"Good news. Sjvek will help me find Prince Daniel. But we have a new problem. He says the battle between the Saurians and us is a plan of the dragons…"

Not all dragons.

"Sorry. It is a plan by a select few dragons. It is their plan to let the humans and Saurians destroy each other. We need to stop the war."

"Dragons are intelligent?" Jordan asked.

Markos smiled. "Even more than the Saurians. Jordan, you will want to meet with the other half of your team before the King returns to Lansing. He will most likely also be imprisoned if caught by the Council. The Troit is the safest city for him to go to. After that, do your best to free the Princess. Sister Elizabeth and Sister Abigael, try a more diplomatic approach to get the Princess released. If anything, they should not deny you access to see how she is doing."

Ready? Markos thought to Sjvek.

Sjvek lowered himself and Markos climbed on.

"Markos, what are you doing!" Sister Elizabeth asked worriedly.

"Going to find Daniel," Markos said as he smiled and winked.

Markos held onto Sjvek's neck. The young dragon flapped his wings to rise from the ground. He left the five humans watching in awe. Markos could not help but smile. This had to be a sight.

We will need to get the saddle.

Sjvek twisted his body slightly side to side. *What's wrong? You do not want to fall?*

Ha, a sense of humor even. Yes, I feel more secure with the saddle.

If those who are searching for me find me, you will need the saddle. Let's hope it does not come to that.

CHAPTER TWENTY-ONE
The Next Generation

"Even a child is known by his doings, whether his work be pure, and whether it be right." – Proverbs 20:11

"In Thee, O Lord, do I put my trust." - Psalms 71:1

H*OW LONG are you able to track somebody this way?*
Around a human month.

Markos was beginning to feel more comfortable communicating with Sjvek telepathically. There were many advantages. Flying, for one. There was no way he could communicate verbally with the dragon flying at some of these tremendous speeds. Bugs were another issue. It was wise to keep one's mouth shut while flying on the back of the dragon for obvious reasons.

Markos sat back and enjoyed the scenery as Sjvek followed an invisible path as he sailed slowly through the air. Markos enjoyed the slow flight the most. Besides being able to relax in the saddle and scan the beauty of the autumn tree colors, it was much warmer than going at the faster speeds. The higher the altitude or the faster Sjvek went, the colder the ride became.

Sjvek turned to the right suddenly, causing Markos to slide far to the left. He had added some ties to the saddle to lock his legs to the side of the dragon. If he hadn't, he would surely be falling to his death right now.

What are you doing?

Other dragons are headed this way. I changed direction so we would not cross paths. They have modified their direction to match our new course. I would advise that I drop you off so you do not get hurt.

Not a chance, Sjvek. You are in this trouble because of me. I will always be here to help.

Korj is the largest of the dragons. I will not be able to defend against him, and you certainly won't be able to either.

Markos leaned forward and tapped the young dragon's side. *This Korj may be big, but I am protected by one that is bigger. There will be many surprises in store for those who chase you.*

Sjvek turned abruptly again. *They are flanking us, more come from the south. Five altogether. Markos, I do not know what to do. Dragons have never fought against dragons.*

Do not be afraid, for God is with us. Turn and face them head on.

Sjvek tilted his body to the left and slowly modified his course.

Now let's go. Faster. Faster. You've gone faster than this. We must meet them as fast as you can.

Markos drew his body closer to the dragon. Sjvek accelerated. The ground below flew by and the wind whipped violently over his back. He was proud of the young dragon.

Markos…prepare. Here they come. 5, 4…

Markos could feel Sjvek's muscles tense as they braced for impact. The young dragon did not waver from his course. He trusted Markos. He flew headstrong straight ahead.

3, 2, 1…

Markos heard *thuds* as the two invisible dragons flew unknowingly into the invisible force field that Markos projected. Markos had used this tactic with Duke previously, and he was glad to see that it worked with the dragon.

The two invisible dragons roared in pain and materialized as they fell toward the Earth. Markos watched as the two dragons fell for a few seconds before they caught themselves and began to pursue Sjvek again. It was obvious which dragon was Korj. The giant black dragon was twice the size of Sjvek.

Climb as fast as you can. How far are the other three?

They will be upon us in one minute.

Markos looked back as the two dragons followed Sjvek upwards on his new course. *You have the speed. Climb as high as you can, then follow what is in my mind.*

Markos watched as the Earth quickly faded away behind them. The air was becoming frigid and thinner, making it hard for Markos to breathe. Sjvek slowed and paused, then turned his body into a dive toward the two advancing dragons. Sjvek folded his wings next to his body and accelerated as if he were an arrow shot from a bow. Markos could not look forward because they were moving so fast. All he could do was hug the back of the dragon and telepath instructions to Sjvek.

Sjvek followed the suggestions. As he approached the attacking dragons, he turned his body upside-down and dove belly to belly with the giant black dragon. Sjvek stuck his claws out and scratched the black dragons belly as they sped past each other. Sjvek kept his wings tucked close to his body and dove faster toward the Earth.

Markos heard the dragon roar in pain and anger as it turned and dove to follow them.

They are gaining speed. Where are the other three?

They are almost here, but their path is not directed at me, they are...

Sjvek was interrupted by the roars of multiple dragons. Sjvek slowed and Markos looked toward the sound. The two dragons that had chased Sjvek were now fiercely defending themselves from a barrage of claws and fire blasts from the three new dragons.

What is going on? Markos asked.

The dragons have split up. Some now follow my mother and the others now have chosen to follow...me. I have caused a civil war among the dragons.

No, Sjvek, Your mother did. She has tricked the world into war and you have shown us all the truth.

Korj blasted the three dragons with a large stream of fire. The three dragons were thrust backwards by the force of the blast. Although the dragons were not burned, Markos saw smoke rise from their bodies.

Hang on. They cannot take another round of that.

Sjvek flapped his wings and whipped his tail to gain momentum. Korj drew his head and neck back and quickly released another blast of fire at the three dragons. Markos was shocked to see the flames abruptly stop and burst in all directions against an invisible wall.

Sjvek flew alongside the other three dragons, and together they all blew fire at the two attackers. Korj and the other dragon were forced to retreat from the battery. The two dragons flew off toward the southern horizon as Sjvek and the other three dragons flapped their wings and watched them retreat.

The four dragons turned in the opposite direction and descended toward an open area on the ground. Markos studied the other dragons as they flew downward. He never imagined being so close to such beautiful and intelligent creatures. The three new dragons were all larger than Sjvek, and they were covered in blue, green, and red scales respectively. Markos wondered how many different colors of dragons there were.

Ten, Sjvek thought to Markos.

Ten what?

Dragons are made up of ten different colors.
They just heard that?
Yes.

Markos could not help but blush. The dragons descended and landed together in a grassy plain.
Markos slid from the back of Sjvek. The dragons were
clearly communicating with each other. Sjvek stomped
his foot and roared at the other dragons. Markos was
startled by the aggressive move, and he jumped back.
He carefully watched what was happening.

Do not be frightened.
What is happening?
They ask why I would submit myself to be subser-
vient to a human. I explained it more as a partnership. I
explained I would not have thought of the tactics I used
against Korj without your help.
And the roaring?
It is a dragon thing. It would be hard to explain
in human terminology. I am their leader. They have the
option of choosing my way or my mother's.
And?
We are not dead are we? They will allow a person
of your choosing to guide them in battles, just as you have

done with me.

Markos was caught off guard. He had not expected that other dragons would allow other humans to ride them. But it made sense. If the dragons had never fought before, who better to teach them than humans who had been fighting for ages. But choosing which humans was an enormous responsibility. It would not be a simple decision.

Markos looked up at the dragons. It was an amazing sight and an incredible feeling to have four dragons surrounding him.

Sjvek knelt to the ground.

We must go. Our mission is not yet complete.

Markos climbed onto the back of Sjvek and strapped himself into the saddle. Sjvek flapped his wings and ascended into the air. Markos watched as the three dragons flew off in the direction from which they came. Then all three turned invisible and Markos could not see them anymore.

CHAPTER TWENTY-TWO
The Long Journey

"Finally, all of you, live in harmony with one another; be sympathetic, love as brothers, be compassionate and humble." – I Peter 3

"If you want to make peace, you don't talk to your friends. You talk to your enemies." - Moshe Dayan (1915-1981)

I ZIKAR PUSHED Daniel's arm. "Stop touching me, you filthy human."

"It is not like I have a choice. You think I want to touch your slimy hand?!" Daniel shouted back at Izikar.

Izikar led Daniel in a westerly direction next to a river running through the woods. He slipped on a rock, causing Daniel to catch his footing to avoid falling with the Saurian.

"You are touching me again, human," Izikar said as he knelt in the water.

"Fine," Daniel replied. He dropped Izikar into the water.

Izikar spoke something unintelligible, and then yanked Daniel down into the water. Human and Saurian rolled in the water while throwing punches at each other's face.

"Well, well, what do we have here?"

Daniel and Izikar stopped fighting. They lay on their backs and turned toward the voice. They looked up and saw four humans.

"Looks like a couple of noblemen playing in the water, boys," one of the men laughed.

"We do not have anything to offer. I would advise you to leave," Daniel said.

The man stepped on Daniel's chest and pinned him down in the shallow water. "You have some nice clothes, and this one has some nice armor. That will do fine."

Daniel quickly wrapped his legs around the man's knees and pulled him into the water. He and Izikar stood in unison with swords ready. Daniel stepped on the man's throat and held him in place. With enough pressure he could kill the man. He hoped it would not come to that.

As one of the other men began to draw his sword, Daniel slapped the top of the man's hand with his sword. Izikar knocked the other two men to the ground with his tail. Daniel lowered his sword toward the man he held in the water and released the man's throat.

"I will say it again. Leave," Daniel said.

The man nodded with wide eyes. Daniel released the man and he quickly scrambled toward the other two.

"Go!" Daniel shouted. The men ran off into

the woods.

"You are such a grand species, aren't you? Feeding on the helpless. Do you kill your young as well?" Izikar asked.

"Not all humans are like that. Do not judge all of us by a few. Your species is not so perfect either. That female Saurian and you are quite different."

Izikar growled. "Human sympathizers. A despicable group. If they met more humans like that," Izikar said, pointing his sword in the direction of the men, "they would understand how detestable your kind really is. Now put your sword away so we can get going."

"No, put your sword away first."

"And have you act like the animal you are and stab me?"

"Fine, we put them away together."

Each man carefully watched the other as they slowly placed their swords back into their scabbards.

"How much farther?"

"At this speed, I calculate about a day."

"Then let's get going. The sooner I am separated from you, the better."

"Then stick out your arm and I will cut off your hand so we can be done with it," Izikar said.

"Why don't you stick out your slimy neck and I will make the world a better place?" Daniel replied.

Daniel and Izikar grabbed each other and fell back to the ground, punching at each other again.

* * * *

DANIEL PULLED IZIKAR'S ARM, causing the Saurian to stop suddenly.

"What do you think you are doing, human?"

"That is a farmhouse. I want to see if they might be able to supply food if anybody is still there."

Daniel looked across the grass plain toward the white farmhouse. He was hungry and thirsty. A barn stood across the dirt road leading to the house and a broken wooden fence encompassed a large open patch of land surrounding the barn. Daniel could not see any farm animals which he knew was not a good sign.

"Fine. This better not be some trick, human."

"It looks abandoned. Do you not have to eat?"

"Of course. Do I look like a rock? I do not know how you humans have survived for so long. Do I not breathe. Of course I have to eat."

Daniel shook his head and began walking toward the farmhouse stopping Izikar in his tirade. He had been forced to listen to the arrogant speech of the Saurian for the whole day and he was getting used to it. As Prince of Rembelshem, he had dealt with many human leaders who were just as arrogant, but only for short periods of time. After dealing with the Saurian, he would gladly deal with the pompous humans.

They approached the house from the dirt road and entered the pathway leading to the house. The front door was slightly open and Daniel cautiously entered first. Brown and orange leaves were scattered throughout the door entryway and were blown further across the wooden floor as Daniel opened the door.

"Hello?" Daniel called out.

"What are you doing, human?" Izikar spat.

"It is proper to announce one's entrance into another's home. You are more likely to be shot by a crossbow bolt otherwise."

"Hello. Anyone home?" Daniel called and entered further into the house.

As Daniel had expected nobody answered. The door had been open for a considerable amount of time and he was sure they would not find anyone living there. He just hoped they did not find anyone *not living* there either. From the lack of farm animals, Daniel figured the previous owners had fled from the location.

Daniel could see the kitchen to the right and pulled the reluctant Saurian deeper into the house. Daniel opened the kitchen pantry and was forced to back away from the smell. Izikar began speaking in the Saurian language, but Daniel did not need to comprehend it to have an idea of what he was saying. The Saurian's sense of smell was far greater than humans'. If the smell was bad for Daniel, it was far worse for Izikar. Daniel almost chuckled at the thought his human short comings finally paid off. After a few moments of letting the smell dissipate, Daniel approached the pantry again.

"What are you doing!?" Izikar shouted, covering his nose.

"It is just some spoiled vegetables," Daniel said, pointing to the unrecognizable, mold-covered mass.

Many jars filled the pantry and Daniel took a couple and sat at the four chair square table in the middle of the kitchen. Izikar stood momentarily but finally sat as well. Daniel looked behind Izikar.

"Must be hard to sit in human chairs with the tail. Do Saurian chairs have backs?"

"No. And if they do, they are modified to fit our needs. I thought you were hungry? If not, let us keep moving."

Daniel opened the two jars and held one to Izikar who cringed his nose and shook his head.

"Apples and peaches," Daniel said with a shrug and began eating sliced pieces from the jars.

Halfway through his jar of apples the front door opened quickly and both men jumped from the table with swords in hand. Daniel smiled when the soft patters against the hard wood floor turned into a gold-colored, medium-sized dog. The two men waited for an owner but none followed. The two men put their weapons away and sat down at the table.

"Come here, boy," Daniel said, patting his leg.

The dog quickly walked to Daniel and put its head on Daniel's leg. Daniel smiled and rubbed the dog's head.

"You must be getting food from somewhere, you look pretty healthy," Daniel said to the dog.

"It cannot understand you. You humans are less intelligent than we ever thought."

Daniel shook his head. "I know it does not understand me. Do Saurians not have pets?"

"Pets are illogical. You supply much to provide for them and receive nothing in return."

Daniel stroked the dogs head and its tail wagged. "You receive companionship and a friend."

"We are beyond such needs. Now hurry, the sooner I am rid of you the sooner I no longer have to listen to your barbaric ways."

Daniel looked at the golden retriever and smiled. It might not be as intelligent as the Saurian, but Daniel would rather be chained to it than Izikar any day. Daniel stopped petting the dog and refocuses on eating his food. Without receiving the attention from one, the dog sought it from another and laid its head on Izikar's leg. Daniel almost choked in laughter as Izikar's eyes widened in shock.

"Odd. It likes you. Pet its head."

"I will do no such thing," Izikar spat. "Shoo, shoo."

Daniel did not feel as hungry and stood from the table. Izikar followed quickly in order to get the dog's head off his leg. After cleaning, they exited the house and were followed by the golden retriever. It took some encouragement but the dog finally did not follow them. If the dog had not looked well fed Daniel would have thought otherwise. To have the companionship of the dog would have made the trip with Izikar more tolerable. But Daniel knew and smiled. It also would have been enjoyable to watch the Saurian be in discomfort around the dogs presence.

* * * *

"DO YOU HUMANS ever stop talking?"

"All I wanted to know was what humans saw you as."

"They see me as a person with this armor on,

if you really need to know," Izikar replied.

The two men had traveled throughout the night, not trusting each other to stop and sleep. Izikar finally led them to a rocky terrain area and paused at a rocky wall. Daniel could have walked past the cave entrance a thousand times and never knew it existed. He was not sure how Izikar opened the rock slab covering the cave entrance, but he understood how it had never been detected over the years.

Izikar carried a staff lit by a strange source. He held it up to some markings on the wall, and then turned to take a new path into the corridors. Originally the cave looked like all the other caves Daniel had seen. But as they descended deeper into the cave, the natural rock formations began to change into more technologically-created surroundings. Daniel marveled at how the rough natural rock walls turned smooth. After an hour of walking, metallic walls became the foundation of the underground pathway.

Different pathways emerged. Daniel knew he would never find his way out of the labyrinth Izikar was leading him through. The yellow lights overhead flickered off and on, but Izikar's light staff flooded the tunnel with abundant blue light. Daniel figured that Izikar was finding his way by reading the strange lettering on the walls at each junction. Izikar suddenly pushed Daniel to the side of a wall instead of entering a four-way junction.

"Shhh…," Izikar whispered as he covered his light staff..

Daniel laid a hand on the hilt of his sword. If Izikar was worried, he was worried. He heard the footsteps long before he saw the shadow walking toward them from the tunnel perpendicular to theirs. The lights flickered and blinked back on. The thing paused, and then continued walking. From the sound of the footsteps and the growing shadow, Daniel knew it was something big. Then he saw it; a massive lizard creature walking on two legs, and standing at least eight feet tall. Its head was shaped like Izikar's, but it had a more blunt and human appearance. The creature had to weigh about five hundred pounds. Its body, arms, and legs were massive. The General was a big man, but this creature would easily surpass the General in height and weight.

As the creature stopped at the intersection of

the two tunnels, Daniel gripped his sword tighter. For once in his life he was unsure how effective the sword would be. The giant creature sniffed the air a couple times and then continued walking past the hallway where Izikar and Daniel were hiding.

Izikar waited until the footsteps could no longer be heard, then he released Daniel from the wall.

"What in the world was that?" Daniel asked.

Izikar peeked around the corner and down the hallway where the creature had gone. "A troll," Izikar whispered.

"A troll? Like a fairy tale troll?"

"Yes. Your *fairy* tales are based on a few of them. They found their way to the surface many years ago. Provisions were made so that they cannot accidentally breach the surface again."

"Are they animals?"

"No...human. They have roughly your intelligence. The Queen decided to leave them here until we have a location for them on the surface."

"You purposely left intelligent beings down here? And you call humans barbaric?"

Izikar snorted and mumbled something that

Daniel did not understand. Izikar hurriedly pulled Daniel down the tunnel from which the troll had come and started through another maze of tunnels. Some opened into rooms with objects that Daniel did not recognize. The inventor part of Daniel wanted to stay and learn about all the multi-colored lights and the multitude of sounds, but Izikar continued dragging him onward.

Izikar finally stopped at the end of a large spacious room. He slid open a glass door to reveal a large enclosed compartment. "Get in."

Daniel got in and sat on one side of the bubble-like contraption, and Izikar sat on the other. Izikar pushed a couple multi-colored buttons that beeped. The glass door closed and shut Daniel and Izikar inside. Suddenly, they began to move.

Daniel forced himself to breathe. He felt like he was stuck in a moving glass coffin with a Saurian. Daniel gripped the seat as the device began to accelerate.

"Relax, human. We have about an hour."

"How far are we going that it takes an hour at this speed?"

"Our final destination is past what you call the Rocky Mountains."

"That is amazing. That takes us a week or more by horse."

"Yes, I know. Maybe now you will understand that you humans have no chance of winning your battles against us. We are far smarter and we have more advanced equipment than you will ever have."

"Humans have the numbers and the will to survive. Your advantage of surprise is gone. In the end you will lose," Daniel replied.

"It is futile to rebel against us, human."

"You have not even seen the beginning of what we *humans* are capable."

Both men remained silent for a long time after that. Daniel watched out the window as they sped through the inside of the Earth.

"So you lived in these two locations...or are there more?"

Daniel was shocked by what he thought was a smile from Izikar. "Silly human. You have no understanding of the magnitude of my people. We have cities spread under the whole Earth. At this very moment every human country on this planet is close to encountering the same peril that your countries have encountered."

The new information whirled in Daniel's mind. He had not even considered that the Saurians may also be attacking the European and Asian countries. Only in the last hundred years had contact been re-established with the new governments of those continents. Both the European and Asian continents had undergone similar transformations of new governments and countries — just as the countries of Rembelshem, Dangaria, and The Republic had divided what was known as the United States. Daniel had never understood just how advanced the Saurian people were until now. It explained how their weapons were lighter and stronger than his own. As strange as it sounded, he knew there was only one way to defeat the Saurians, and that was to unite as one force against their common enemy. The humans had the numbers against the Saurians, and they needed to use that to their advantage.

The lights in the tunnel dimmed as the vehicle slowed until it gradually stopped in absolute darkness.

"I guess this is not what usually happens," Daniel said.

"Of course not, human. Give it a second."

The two men sat silently for a few minutes, waiting for the power to return. Daniel laughed in the darkness. Being trapped a mile under the surface in a pitch black tunnel with a Saurian had just reached the top of his never-want-to-do list.

"Is there something funny, human? I find the situation far from hilarious."

"This contraption will begin moving again once your fireless lights come back on."

"And what if it does not? What then?"

"Then we walk if need be."

"Just get up and walk hundreds of miles in utter blackness. Absolutely illogical."

"You have not even seen a glimpse of the human will to survive."

Daniel felt shaking through his handcuff and it finally occurred to him. "You do not like the dark do you?"

"Shut up, human."

"But that doesn't make sense. It would be *illogical* for you to be afraid of the dark."

"Of course it does not make sense. But ever since I fell down a drainage pipe when I was younger, it is so."

The lights in the tunnel flickered and the vehicle began to move again. Daniel could actually see the relief on Izikar's face as they began to accelerate.

"Do not say another word, human."

Daniel was silent for the remainder of the ride. The glass vehicle began to slow. It stopped in a large cavernous room similar to the one they had started in.

Izikar exited the vehicle and yanked Daniel out. Daniel was irritated, and he pulled back on his chained arm to stop Izikar's momentum.

"Filthy human, you try my patience. We have almost reached our objective."

"Knock off the pulling on my arm then."

Izikar turned his head toward a noise coming from one of the open tunnels leading from the large room. Daniel heard the noise too. Another troll was coming.

"Come," Izikar said.

Izikar hurriedly led Daniel from the room into one of the side corridors. Izikar stopped in front of some doors and pushed the lit buttons next to them. The door slid open to reveal a room. Izikar entered and Daniel was forced to follow before the door slid shut behind them.

Daniel looked around. The room was obviously a living quarters of some kind. There was a strange couch, a couple of chairs, and some tables. He had never thought about the Saurians having such places. They were either trying to kill him, or he was killing them. Seeing such a room reminded Daniel that they were not just creatures, but intelligent beings with necessities as humans.

Izikar led Daniel into a small room that appeared to be a study. There was odd-looking equipment on the desk. Izikar opened a drawer. He pulled out a small metal stick and stuck it into their metal handcuffs. The handcuffs clicked open, releasing the two enemies.

Daniel rubbed his arm. He was glad to be free from the contraption.

"That is it?" Daniel asked.

"Stupid human," Izikar said, holding up the pencil-like object. "Do you have any clue…? Never mind. Your simpleton mind will never understand such technological concepts. We must go. I will lead you out of these dwellings. After that, our treaty is over. If I see you again, you will die."

"I cannot wait for the day that you try."

CHAPTER TWENTY-THREE
Enemies Unite

"'But I say unto you, Love your enemies, bless them that curse you, do good to them that hate you, and pray for them which despitefully use you, and persecute you.'" – Matthew 5:44

"Am I not destroying my enemies when I make friends of them?" - Abraham Lincoln (1809 - 1865)

M ARKOS HUNG onto the saddle as Sjvek glided through some turbulence. He relaxed as the flight smoothed out.

You are quite smaller than the other dragons. Is that based on your age or coloring?

Age. I am what you would call a human teenager, and the other three were adults.

Yet, you are their leader?

The dragons follow a hereditary monarchy. My grandfather passed the leadership to my mother and now the new sect of dragons follows me accordingly.

And if you and your mother were to die?

Let's hope that does not happen.

Agreed.

We should be arriving at the location that is as far as I can take you. The Human and Saurian will soon exit the rocky hills to the north.

Saurian?

They have been traveling together for a considerable amount of time. For the most part, they moved rather quickly, but there were also many times that they rolled around in the ground together. That part does not make sense to me.

Just one Saurian? If he is walking, Daniel is co-herent and not drugged. He could have easily taken out the single Saurian. They are exiting?

Yes, soon. There is a tunnel leading deep within the earth from a hidden entrance between two boulders. Their thoughts are becoming clearer, so I know they are coming closer to the surface. Both are alive, but both are undecided about what to do after they leave the tunnel. They may fight, they may leave peacefully. From what I gather, it could easily go either way.

Let's make that decision for them, Markos thought to Sjvek.

* * * *

DANIEL WATCHED the Saurian's every move. He knew he could not trust him. Although Izikar seemed sincere in saying he would let Daniel leave without incident, it was hard for Daniel to believe. The Saurians were all bloodthirsty killers without emotions. Or were they?

Daniel did not know. His emotions bounced between wondering if there was more to the Saurians than he first thought and wanting to kill them all. If Izikar did not make an offensive move, Daniel would fulfill the agreement and go his own separate way. Then Daniel was torn. How could he just let the leader of those who were killing his people go. He could win a giant battle against the Saurians with just one swing of his sword.

The rocky tunnel that they were following ended abruptly at a rock wall. Izikar touched a device on the wall and the rock door slid open. *This is it. Time to see if the Saurians are creatures of honor or not.*

Daniel cautiously walked through the door, and Izikar followed. The rock door slid shut with a *thud*.

It was early evening. The sun was beginning to set. They had entered the cave before lunch, so the thought that they had traveled to the other side of the continent and back in less than six hours was incomprehensible to Daniel. The whole experience had been surreal. Daniel snapped back to reality as he noticed the sun was blotted out, and a huge shadow covered both of them.

Daniel looked up in disbelief. Dragons were

not real! But there was one hovering above them. Then it roared. The ground rumbled, and Daniel was forced to cover his ears. He first thought was it was a Saurian trick, but a quick glance at Izikar's face proved that the Saurian was just as shocked. Izikar punched at the rock wall to re-open the door. Both men drew their weapons and stood side-by-side facing the dragon. Two little swords would not do much harm to a dragon, but it was all they had.

"Open the door!" Daniel shouted.

Izikar reluctantly turned his back to the creature and began pushing on the rock's surface. Daniel took a defensive stance between the dragon and Izikar. The dragon landed on the ground twenty feet away and folded its wings. Daniel was surprised to see a man slide from the dragon's back and land gracefully on the ground. From his clothing, Daniel knew exactly who it was.

"Markos?"

Markos patted the dragon's side, and then approached the two men. Izikar stopped what he was doing and turned.

"What is this?! A human trick to kill me?"

Izikar said, holding his sword defensively.

Izkar, hold!

Daniel was confused, and he could tell Izikar was also. Nobody's mouth had moved, but he heard the male voice in his head.

"This is not possible. You cannot have such abilities!"

Markos continued to walk forward. Izikar leaped at Markos with his sword, but he was picked up while in mid-air and tossed against the rock wall. Izikar was held two feet off the ground for a few seconds and then was released by the invisible force.

Izikar'Etra Sandamung'So you have been deceived, as have all of us. If you attack again, it will be your last.

Daniel knew Izikar had also heard the unspoken words. He knew it was not Markos, but… Daniel turned to eye the dragon.

Yes, Daniel Lancaster, I am an intelligent being and not a dumb animal.

"And actually, the dragons are far smarter than either the Saurians or Humans," Markos added.

"Preposterous," Izikar spat.

The dragon began flooding their minds with equations. As an inventor, Daniel was very adept with mathematics, but the equations the dragon filled his mind with were far beyond his comprehension.

"It can't be," Izikar said in disbelief.

"It is true, Izikar. Your queen has been tricked into this war by the dragons to let the Humans and Saurians destroy each other. The consequences of their actions have not only cost many human and Saurian lives, but now the dragons have split into factions and are at war with each other. You both have shown that you can forget your hostility toward each other and join forces when facing a common enemy. I tell you now, you have a common enemy, and we must stop this war between our races."

"The battle of Lansing is done. We'll have time to worry about the war later. What about Rebekah?"

"I hate to be the one to tell you this, but with you, Rebekah, and Robert missing, the King's Council has taken over Rembelshem. I unknowingly delivered Rebekah right to the council. She has been imprisoned."

"What!? Markos, how could you? Why have

you not freed her?"

"The coup has been secret. Not even the city knows. You know I would tear down the palace to free her if I could, but that would break the Paladin treaty, and I cannot do that."

Daniel kicked the dirt. He wanted to explode. Coup or no coup, he would deal with the counselors when he returned to Lansing. He had failed over and over again to do his one duty and protect his daughter. She had been imprisoned and enslaved, and he had been helpless to do anything about it. The horrors she had had to go through without him being there. At every turn where he got close to her, something else happened to pull him away.

"The greatest problem is not Rebekah. The main problem at hand is that the Council has dispatched the Rembelshem army against the advancing Saurian army."

Daniel looked to Izikar for confirmation.

"We had no plans to attack this soon. Your information must be incorrect."

I can confirm the information. I overheard my mother saying the final battle was about to commence.

After that, her plans were to kill all surviving Saurians and Humans.

"Your mother?" Izikar and Daniel asked in unison.

Yes. I believe my mother has been planning this for many years with your queen. Because of this, I am now at war with my own mother and those that follow her.

Daniel looked at Izikar and watched him closely. "You knew of this, didn't you?"

"Not exactly. But the new information fit the missing pieces of a puzzle that I have been working on. I have suspected there was an outside influence, but I have not been able to prove it."

"You two have the power to stop this war. In a week the two forces will collide and tens of thousands of humans and Saurians will die needlessly. Sjvek will lead the dragons that follow him and keep the armies separated. The dragon numbers are limited, so they will be taking a great risk."

"What if we had another army to help the dragons keep the two armies separated?" Daniel said with a sly smile.

Both Markos and Izikar looked at Daniel, confused.

"The trolls. What if we took the trolls to the battle?"

"Trolls?" Markos asked.

Daniel raised his hand above his head. "Eight foot trolls. The Saurians left them in the caverns below. Not as smart as the Saurians, but as smart as humans. He says they are there to protect their underground cities, but I think the Saurians are embarrassed by them and left them on purpose."

"That is not true. They would have made an excellent addition to my army. The choice to leave them was made by the Queen herself. Your idea is worthy though, even for a human. A thousand trolls marching into the middle of the battlefield would make both humans and Saurians pause."

Just to make a point, I believe it would have been my mother's plan to leave these trolls behind. In doing so, she instantly negated the biggest threat that the dragons would have to deal with after the Saurian and Human war.

Daniel looked at Izikar and Izikar nodded in agreement. "It would answer my questions on the topic perfectly."

"Then we agree. You will get the trolls and we will gather the dragons. Hopefully we can stop a war that should never have started. Daniel, I instructed Special Forces Officer Jordan to free Rebekah if he can. He was injured and not able to continue the whole mission. The others successfully freed your brother and the other human slaves," Markos said.

"Impossible! No human would have been able to make it past the Psi'Drakor."

"I assume the Psi'Drakor are the invisible Saurians? I hate to inform you that they are not as invincible as you might think. I witnessed their destruction by the hand of one human."

Izikar's lip curled into a snarl. "Jarod the Great."

Markos looked shocked. "Yes, actually. You know of him?"

"How could I not have heard of the human who was rumored to have killed fifty of my men single-handedly? And now you say he is able to see and kill the Psi'Drakor?" Izikar shook his head in frustration.

"Markos, you must be mistaken. It could not have been Jarod. I trained the boy, and I know there is no way he could have achieved everything that has been rumored. He is just a boy pretending to be something he is not. He put my daughter's life in jeopardy by participating in her rescue mission. When I find him I will prove that he is nothing more than the scrawny boy he is."

"You will need to stand in line, human. When I find him, I will prove to my people that a single human cannot do what has been rumored."

Markos chuckled, causing the two men to look at him. "You both will want to check your egos. The both of you combined will not be able to defeat him. I have watched him in battle, and one higher than all of us guides him.

We are wasting time. You have one week to bring the trolls to the battle. Sjvek and I must also go. The dragons are spread out across the continent and we must hurry to make the deadline as well." Markos reached out, and then he and Daniel locked forearms. "Until the next time."

Markos released Daniel's arm and bowed toward Izikar. "Izikar. I hope this is a new beginning between our kinds."

Izikar bowed his head to Markos.

Daniel watched in amazement as Markos climbed fearlessly onto the back of the dragon. The dragon ascended and began flapping its wings. It climbed swiftly. *Markos and a dragon*, Daniel thought. *I can't wait to hear how that story began.*

Daniel looked at Izikar. "Ready?"

"Of course I am ready, human. I am not the one who is intellectually behind," Izikar said. He began pushing areas on the rock wall to open the door.

Oh, this was going to be another fun trip, Daniel thought as he followed Izikar into the tunnels.

CHAPTER TWENTY-FOUR
Trolls

"When a resolute young fellow steps up to the great bully, the world, and takes him boldly by the beard, he is often surprised to find it comes off in his hand, and that it was only tied on to scare away the timid adventurers."   - Ralph Waldo Emerson (1803 - 1882)

DANIEL FOLLOWED as Izikar led the way through the maze of metal corridors again. An hour ago, Daniel would have gladly swung his sword through the back of the creature's neck. Now he had no choice but to honor the unspoken treaty between the two men. Daniel needed Izikar to gather the army of trolls and help lead them to the battlefield. Being among so many of his enemies would put Daniel in a serious predicament. Daniel knew he could win one-to-one against Izikar. If a problem escalated between him and the Saurians during the journey, winning would not be possible.

Even if they succeeded in stopping the war instigated by the dragons, Daniel doubted that the struggles between the two species would end. The rift had already been created. Each side abhorred the other. Daniel knew the human species. Even without a war, many of the humans could not tolerate the Saurians' existence, and they would create problems.

Daniel understood their feelings well. He had spent the last six months killing every Saurian that had crossed his path. The vile creatures had separated him from his daughter and destroyed thousands of human lives. Daniel became agitated as he thought about all that the creatures had done.

"Listen, human. I do not know how the trolls will react to a human in their presence. I advise you to let me do the talking."

"I am curious. Why did we hide from them previously?"

"Because I did not want to explain to them that I was not there to free them. They would have been filled with rage, and they would have killed us on the spot."

"Rage? I thought Saurians did not have many emotions?"

"The trolls are not as logical as the rest of us. They have… human-like emotions," Izikar said disgustedly.

"Really, this should be interesting."

Izikar finally stopped in the large chamber with the glass vehicle. He walked over to a metal console with several colored buttons that were lit. He began speaking the Saurian language into a device. The Saurian's voice, amplified by the device, echoed from the top of the room and throughout the corridors. Daniel covered his ears. The Saurian speech was awful in the first place, but magnified it was horrendous. Daniel knew they were coming. The hammering of several large boots on the metal floor thundered from all five of the corridors that led into the chamber.

Daniel backed himself against a wall. He really did not want to get trampled. When the first troll arrived he looked similar to the one Daniel had seen before. When the second troll arrived, Daniel was startled. For some reason it had never occurred to him that there were female trolls.

Daniel had never been intimidated by a female in his life. That was, until now. The female troll stood almost as tall as her male counterpart, and Daniel estimated she was four hundred pounds of muscle. There was no way he could block a direct swing from her. She would bust his sword and bury her weapon half-way through him.

More male and female trolls arrived, and the large room filled up quickly. The situation was starting to make Daniel feel very uncomfortable. There were at least a hundred trolls now in the room; each one capable of doing great bodily harm with one swing of a giant fist.

Many of them had noticed him, but few paid attention to him. Why should they? He was a tiny speck amongst them. As they talked amongst themselves, their primary attention was focused on Izikar. Daniel was amused that Izikar looked so nervous.

Izikar pushed a button on the console and spoke into the device again. His voice blared again throughout the room. As Izikar continued talking, Daniel watched as the trolls became agitated. Very agitated.

Daniel side-stepped along the wall toward Izikar.

"What did you say to them?"

"I told them the truth, human. I am here to release them in exchange for their assistance, but once we're done, they will return here."

"You what?!" Daniel yelled. "You would lock them back in here? For being so smart, you Saurians are stupid."

"I have no choice, human. Without the Queen's approval they must return here until her decision is made."

"Think, Izikar. The rules do not apply any more. Your Queen has been compromised. What she decrees may no longer be good for your kind. Do they speak my language?"

"Of course. Most of your languages."

Daniel pushed Izikar to the side and stepped in front of the console. He pushed the button and spoke into the device.

"Ladies and gentle…" Daniel paused and looked at the crowd of towering trolls. This might be harder than he thought.

"Greetings one and all. My name is Prince Daniel Lancaster of Rembelshem. The Saurians," Daniel said as he made a hand gesture toward Izikar, "have destroyed most of the human lands. They have also killed thousands of my people. To stand here next to one of them is not easy. But, for the survival and safety of my people, I must. The Saurians and humans have been tricked into a war against one another by the dragons. They are far more intelligent than we first believed. As we speak, the humans and Saurians march forward to fight the final battle. Many lives will be lost. And once that is done, neither side will be prepared to counter the attack that the dragons have planned. Their goal is to destroy every human and Saurian that is left after the battle. You were left behind for a reason. The dragons do not want you on the surface. If you do not fight, their job is much easier. And when all Saurians on the surface are dead, who is left to free you? No one. The dragons would rule the Earth. But with your help, we have a chance to stop this upcoming war between the humans and Saurians. With your help, we have a much greater chance to defeat the dragons. I give you my promise here and now, as the Prince of Rembelshem, that no matter what your superiors say, you will not be forced back here. If need be, you will have political asylum within the human boundaries. Humans may not be as smart as the Saurians, but we do have compassion.

Murmurs rose from the crowd of trolls.

"Now get them ready and do not mess it up again," Daniel said to Izikar as he stepped away from the console.

Daniel was amused by the look that Izikar gave him. The Saurian had just been shown up by a human, and he was not happy about it. If the trolls were similar emotionally to humans, the dry logical approach the Saurians had would not work. As princes, he and his brother had spent hours and hours training to deliver speeches; the proper hand movements and the proper emphasis on certain words. Giving a speech was an art form in itself.

Izikar spoke into the device, and then the trolls hurriedly left the room while conversing with one another.

"Come, human. We will meet them on the surface."

Daniel followed Izikar and smiled mischievously. For one who was *unemotional*, Izikar sure seemed mad.

* * * *

"HA!" Daniel shouted in triumph.

The troll that sat across the makeshift table from Daniel groaned in defeat and tossed his game pieces onto the table. It had taken two days for all the trolls throughout the underground chambers to gather their armor, weapons, and food. As they waited at a temporary camp on the surface, Daniel had begun to learn more about the trolls. He was finding the trolls far more personable than Izikar, who kept himself apart from the others. He was intrigued by a game that some had been playing to pass the time, and he finally asked more about it. It had taken multiple losses, but he had finally won his first match.

"Lucky, human," Gorj said.

"Maybe humans are not stupid after all. Or maybe Gorj is not as smart as humans," said one of the trolls who was looking on, which caused an eruption of laughter.

"At least the humans will play and lose, unlike the *Stones*," Gorj said as he nodded his head toward Izikar. This was not the first time the trolls had used the slang to refer to the Saurians. Stones was a reference to the Saurians' lack of emotions. He was beginning to like the trolls more and more. Gorj bent over the table and whispered, "You know why they do not like to play games? It is not because they think it is *illogical*, but because they do not like to lose. Games of luck drive them crazy because they try to figure out all the possibilities instead of just enjoying the game."

Daniel smiled. "Is that why this game is more popular than a more *logical* one? To annoy the Stones?"

Gorj smiled a huge fanged grin. "You are smarter than I expected. But I cannot confirm or deny that accusation."

Daniel smiled. Never in his life would he have thought that he would be sitting at a table across from a Saurian with a head twice the size of his, and fangs the length of his fingers. If he would have encountered one in the woods, he would have run or tried to fight it. He would have thought it was a monster and never imagined it would have intelligence.

Izikar conversed with a troll as he approached. "All have exited. It is time to move."

Daniel stood and stretched. They only had three days left to reach the estimated time of battle. They would have to move hard and fast. Daniel jumped onto a three-foot boulder, which allowed him to see over the top of many heads. As far as he could see there were trolls standing, talking, or dismantling tents. Now they all were wearing chain mail and armor, and they had a variety of weapons strapped to their backs or hips. He understood why the dragons did not want to deal with the trolls. They were a formidable enemy. One thousand trolls could easily match a human force of ten thousand men.

Daniel jumped off the boulder. They needed to hurry. There was a war to stop, his daughter to free, and the Council to deal with.

CHAPTER TWENTY-FIVE
Captured

"So that we may boldly say, The Lord is my helper, and I will not fear what man shall do unto me." - Hebrews 13:6

"Hereby perceive we the love of God, because he laid down his life for us: and we ought to lay down our lives for the brethren." - I John 3:16

J AROD SCANNED the horizon. He and Billy were scouting the path a half mile in front of the others. They walked down the main dirt road that ran through an open field of dead grass. The morning was brisk, and sporadic patches of snow covered the field and road. Jarod wrapped his black leather Special Forces trench coat tighter around himself. He hoped the impending snowstorm would hold off until they reached Lansing. The country's leaders did not have sufficient clothing to protect themselves if the weather turned colder.

There it was again. Jarod raised his hand and the group paused. He did not know what it was or how he knew, but something was in the wide open field with them. The change in the field had been so minor and subtle. A piece of knee-high dried grass had moved, or it might have been a scrape against the ground to the right of them. Jarod drew his swords and Billy followed his lead.

From ten feet off the road three men stood up from the tall grass. They had been almost invisible until they stood up. Jarod shook his head and let out a sigh of relief.

Jordan strode forward with a smile and clapped his hands lightly.

"Well done, Jarod. We were sure we were going to have some fun with the rookies. Michael has you scouting?"

Jarod nodded. "You look better, but what brings you out here?"

Jordan grimaced. "We have a problem and need to detour the group. Come, I'll explain more when we reach Michael."

The five Special Forces men hurriedly joined the approaching group. After a quick reunion, Jordan pulled the King and Special Forces aside and explained the situation.

"So you have no idea where Daniel is?" King Robert asked.

"None. He left secretly with a small group and never returned. Paladin Markos is searching for him now with the help of…you would not believe me," Jordan said.

"A dragon?" King Robert asked.

Jordan looked surprised. "Yes, how did you know?"

"We watched him and the dragon fry a few dozen of the critters and then fly the Princess off," Michael answered.

"Well, it's a relief to not have to explain that one. The second half of the problem is that Paladin Markos's dragon said that the war between the lizard creatures and us was initially devised by the dragons. Their plan is to kill all human and Saurian survivors after the war."

The King shook his head. "First things first. I assume you have a plan to free the Princess?"

"Yes. After we safely transport you and the others to the Troit, the team will get the Princess," Jordan answered.

"That is unacceptable. Too much time has transpired already. How are you getting into Lansing?"

Jordan looked at the King, confused. "Through the   gates."

Robert shook his head. "They will be waiting for you. I have a better way in. We will first need to get through the Great Wall guards. They may have been compromised already so we need to continue toward the Outlaw City as planned to avoid alerting the Council. After that, two of your men should be enough to transport the group to the Troit."

"And yourself?"

"Do you know where the secret escape tunnel is that leads out of Lansing? No. Then I will be going with you."

* * * *

JAROD HELD BOTH SWORDS and scanned the surroundings as the group of seven men walked through the long dark tunnel. The King and two others held torches to the light the way, but the rest of the Special Forces had their weapons prepared to attack at the first sign of trouble.

It was amazing to Jarod that such a tunnel existed. The tunnel started in a forest outside the Lansing walls, and the King said it would lead them directly into the Royal Forest located on the third Royal level of Lansing. King Robert said his brother designed and helped create the escape tunnel. The same Prince Daniel who had designed the Special Forces chainmail he was wearing, and the same Prince Daniel who had requested he be part of the mission to free the Princess. Jarod hoped to meet them both someday. The Lancaster family seemed to be full of surprises.

The tunnel was dark and musty, but not full of as many cobwebs as he expected. His questions about the tunnels were answered when the King said the Princess had recently used them multiple times to bring food into Lansing during the siege. The same Princess that the King he was walking with had taken as prisoner. Now the King was working to free her. *Yes, the Lancaster family is definitely an interesting family*, Jarod thought.

Jordan was the first to reach the end wall, where there was a ladder leading to the surface. The flames were doused and the rest of the team encircled the King. Jordan climbed the ladder and pushed the hatch open slightly. Cold air filled the tunnel. He opened the hatch fully and then signaled for everybody to proceed.

The first thing Jarod saw was the Royal Palace towering above the trees only a few hundred yards away. The night air was cold, and the full moon lit the palace and the surroundings. The one inch layer of snow reflected the moonlight, making the night brighter than normal.

Once all the men were out of the tunnel, the King closed the hatch, which was shaped like a tree stump.

Jordan looked at the castle gate through a looking glass.

"There are four guards per gate. We…" Jordan was interrupted by the sound of a crossbow bolt flying past his head.

Eight Council Guards came running through the woods toward them.

"Go, go, go," Jordan shouted to the group.

Jarod pushed the King toward the tunnel exit as Jordan held it open. A guard aimed for the King as he entered the tunnel. Jarod jumped in front of the King. The arrow pierced Jarod's shoulder.

Jordan quickly helped Jarod to the tunnel. More crossbow bolts flew by their heads and struck the trees or skittered across the ground. Jarod shoved Jordan into the tunnel and then jumped behind the fake tree stump for protection. Jordan tried to help Jarod into the tunnel again, but a new barrage of bolts forced the men to hide. Jordan had to climb down into the passageway for protection as the guards approached. Jarod was cornered with his back against the stump as the guards advanced and shot bolts at him. He sat on the ground with his hands open as six guards with loaded crossbows encircled him. There was not much he could do. One wrong move and he would look like a pin cushion. The lead guard stepped forward and hit Jarod in the head with the blunt side of his crossbow, and Jarod's world went black.

CHAPTER TWENTY-SIX
The Council Removed

"Cautious, careful people, always casting about to preserve their reputation and social standing, never can bring about a reform. Those who are really in earnest must be willing to be anything or nothing in the world's estimation, and publicly and privately, in season and out, avow their sympathy with despised and persecuted ideas and their advocates, and bear the consequences." - Susan B. Anthony (1820 - 1906)

J AROD WOKE to complete blackness. He waited a few moments to let his eyes adjust. It did not help much. From the muffled sound of voices and the strange air pressure he felt, he seemed to be in a room made of stone or bricks. He was lying on his back. He carefully felt his left shoulder. Somebody had removed the arrow and bandaged his shoulder. He sat up and took in his surroundings. It was some type of small brick jail cell with one thick wooden door.

He kicked the door. It was extremely thick and solid.

"Good luck with that. I have not had any luck," said a female's voice from the cell next to him.

Jarod kicked the door again. It was not going to move.

Jarod wondered how the female's voice was clearer than he would expect. He searched the wall between the cells and found a square fist-sized opening. Jarod sat on the ground next to the hole.

"I have to agree, ma'am."

"Please call me Rebekah."

Jarod chuckled. Could it be? He already knew

the answer. "As in the Princess Lancaster?"

There was a long pause. "Yes. But nobody knows I am in here. Who is this? You sound very young."

"My name is Jarod, Your Highness."

"Jarod the Great, I presume?"

Jarod blushed. The Princess Lancaster even knew of him. "Yes, Your Highness. Just Jarod, please. I really do not like that name."

"Jarod, it is a pleasure to finally meet you. Your reputation from your deeds on the battlefield precedes you. After witnessing them first hand, I understand why. You are a believer then?"

"I, ah, yes," Jarod stuttered. He was not prepared for such an open question. "King Robert spoke highly of your own faith, Your Highness."

"He did?"

"He said you were willing to die for your faith. I am not sure what you did, but it made a real difference to him."

There was a long pause. "Everything alright, Your Highness?"

"Yes, Jarod. That is some unforeseen, yet very

welcome, news. So what happened, why are you here?"

"Our mission to free you did not go according to plan. I was shot with an arrow to protect the King."

"My uncle? What was he doing here?"

"He led us through the escape tunnels. It was his idea to free you sooner rather than later, Your Highness."

"Amazing. He captured me once, and then he tries to free me."

Jarod laughed. "I am sorry, Princess. I thought the same thing."

Jarod heard slight laughter from the other side of the wall.

"It is funny. Please, just call me Rebekah, Jarod. In this environment, it would make me feel more comfortable. I am sorry you were imprisoned to save me."

"It is not your fault. You did not imprison yourself. You did not start his war, Your High... Rebekah. You remind me of a Rebekah I once knew."

"Oh, really? A girlfriend?" Rebekah's voice teased.

"No, no. She really did not know I was alive. But she was determined, intelligent, and beautiful. I..

uhm.. can't say I have ever seen you, I just hear the confidence in your voice."

"Wow. A crush, huh?" Rebekah joked. "But what of the slave camp? You did not see me then?"

"I saw you, but not in a normal way. It is hard to explain."

"Like seeing the whole world as the molecules they are composed of?"

"Yes! You have experienced it too?"

"Yes, once," Rebekah said softly.

Jarod and Rebekah paused and listened. They heard footsteps coming their way. Jarod could hear a knock on the Princess's door.

"Princess?"

"Yes."

"It is Sister Elizabeth. I am an acquaintance of your uncle, Paladin Markos. The Council has granted me permission to visit. Are they treating you decently?"

"Yes, they are."

"Sister Elizabeth? The same Sister that has Thadius?" Jarod said through the small hole between the cells.

"I…who are you?"

"My name is Jarod, Sister. Jarod the Great, if you remember. I left Thadius with you."

"Thadius? As in a four year-old blonde-haired boy?" Rebekah asked.

"I forgot, you knew Thadius as well, Princess," Sister Elizabeth said.

"Knew?" Jarod asked. He was alarmed.

"Oh, Jarod. I am so sorry to have to tell you like this. After you left, Thadius got really sick. The counselors removed us from the palace, so we did not have access to the proper medicines. He…he… has gone from this world."

Jarod's world crashed in on him. The ever-smiling and happy boy he had watched and protected so carefully was gone. In all he had gone through, Thadius had been his one bright light through it all. Tears flowed from his eyes. On the other side of the wall he could also hear the Princess crying.

"Jarod, give me your hand."

Jarod reached thru the hole with his good arm and the Princess was able to intertwine her fingers around his. They both sat there crying, holding each other's hand.

The counselors…They had restricted Thadius from seeing the doctor. They had locked up the Princess. It was their greed and lust for power that had caused this.

Jarod released the Princess's hand and stood up. He kicked the door. He kicked it again. The room that was once fully dark, turned into full light. He knew what was happening. The tiny white and black particles swirled and vibrated, showing him the door, the walls, and even the outlines of the Princess and Sister Elizabeth beyond.

The counselors…The door stood in his way. Jarod kicked it again, and it exploded against the opposite side of the hall. Sister Elizabeth and the Princess gasped at the tremendous sound. It vibrated throughout the castle. Jarod stepped from his cell and turned toward the Princess's door. Sister Elizabeth was shocked at the sight and stepped out of his way. Jarod pushed against the door. The hinges burst from their sockets, and the heavy door collapsed into the cell.

The counselors…Jarod turned and walked down the hallway away from the women.

"Jarod, you have to stop!" Sister Elizabeth called from behind.

The counselors... Jarod knew where they were. He sensed, almost smelled, their corruption.

Palace guards rushed down the hallway toward him. Most of them paused when they saw him, but others ran the opposite direction. Only a few were brave enough to charge. Jarod fluidly dodged the swings of the swords and counter attacked. He left a line of bodies lying on the ground with broken wrists, knees, and dislocated shoulders. He did not want to kill them, but he made sure that they did not attack him again any time soon.

Rebekah and Sister Elizabeth followed Jarod, tip-toeing through the mangled mess of limbs. A few guards were coherent enough to grab their legs, only to be kicked in the head.

Jarod followed the stairs upward, which led him into the cavernous palace entranceway. Jarod stopped. Sister Elizabeth and Rebekah hurriedly ran up the stairs and paused behind him.

"Halt!" a guard shouted.

Ten guards with crossbows stood at each of

the two large gateways that led out of the palace. Jarod would not have cared about the guards if it were not for the Princess and the Sister. He did not want to leave the palace. His goal was to find the blackness that slithered in the upper western tower.

"Stay here," Jarod commanded, and then he walked into the middle of the chamber.

"Ready, Aim, Fire!"

"Jarod!" Rebekah yelled.

Twenty crossbow bolts flew at Jarod and then ricocheted off an invisible shield.

"He fills his hands with lightning and commands it to strike its mark," Jarod whispered. He was recalling words from his readings.

Winds rushed from outside through the two entryways and swirled into a massive storm inside the building. Lightning struck multiple places, sending guards flying onto the drawbridges. The remaining guards ran out of the palace as the storm began to die down.

Jarod crossed the entranceway and climbed the stairs leading to the western tower.

"Jarod?" Rebekah said.

"Come, Princess. Only death goes that way," Sister Elizabeth said, pulling on Rebekah's arm. She led Rebekah out of the palace.

Jarod followed the stairs until he reached the level where the blackness dwelt. The two guards standing outside the room drew their swords, but they were quickly struck down by Jarod. They lay groaning on the floor.

As Jarod opened the door, he was enveloped by the overpowering smell of fear and evil. The seven council members cowered in their seats at the sight of Jarod. Jarod closed the door behind him.

"The evil taint in this world you have produced will be no more. You are relinquished of your powers," Jarod said.

Jarod closed his eyes as he began to draw all the electrical ions he could mentally grasp into that one room.

* * * *

REBEKAH RAN from the palace behind Sister Elizabeth. The guards were distracted and had not yet reorganized. They had reached the southern marble stairs leading to the residential level when she began to hear it. Rebekah grabbed Sister Elizabeth's arm and they both paused to stare at the Royal Palace as the low hum began to grow louder. The noise became so intense that Rebekah could feel the vibrations in her chest. The wind whistled toward the palace. Suddenly the humming and wind stopped. For that second, all the eyes of Lansing were looking toward the Royal Palace.

Rebekah saw it before she heard it. Three-fourths of the way up the left tower, rocks and debris exploded from the tower and showered across the royal level. It was followed by an immense *boom* that shook all of Lansing.

"Jarod," Rebekah whispered.

"Is alive."

"What was that?" Rebekah asked.

"An example of one who has been given a tremendous amount of power and responsibility. One who is second only to you."

"I…no…" Rebekah said, looking at the billowing dust still pouring from the hole in the tower.

"It is still not safe for you. We will return later," Sister Elizabeth said. She grabbed Rebekah's arm and led her down the marble steps.

CHAPTER TWENTY-SEVEN
The Queen

"Before the mountains were brought forth, or ever thou hadst formed the earth and the world, even from everlasting to everlasting, thou art God."
- Psalms 90:2

"What you always do before you make a decision is consult. The best public policy is made when you are listening to people who are going to be impacted. Then, once policy is determined, you call on them to help you sell it."
- Elizabeth Dole

THERE WAS A KNOCK at the door. Rebekah jumped up from the table holding her sword. She had a right to be jumpy. In the last six months she had been imprisoned three times. She would not let it happen again. Sister Elizabeth said she was more gifted than even Jarod the Great. Rebekah was not sure if she was ready to willingly call upon that power, even to prevent being captured again.

The door opened and Sister Elizabeth and Sister Abigael entered. Rebekah felt relieved as she let her sword tip fall to the ground. As a man entered behind Sister Abigael, Rebekah lifted her sword up again.

"Phillip," Rebekah whispered in distaste. "What is he doing here?"

"Princess, it is alright. He is here to help," Sister Elizabeth said as she placed a hand on the top of Rebekah's sword and pushed it back to the ground.

"I trusted him once and he failed."

"Princess, I do not deny that I failed you. I was a miserable, selfish old man. The General's Grandma led me down a new path. A new path of faith."

No matter what hard feelings she had against the man, there was not much she could do with the sword, so she put it away. She had lived in the same apartment with the man while in the Troit. She had also kicked him out many nights and dumped out his alcohol. She did not stand for it then, and she would not stand for any of it again. One encounter with the *changed* man would not change what she already knew about the man.

It was early morning, the day after Jarod had helped her escape from the Royal Palace prison. The city was abuzz with rumors, so the Sisters had left a few hours earlier to find out the true status of the government.

Phillip stepped forward. "Princess, I am here as a delegate of King Robert inviting you to return to the palace to fulfill your rightful position as Princess of Rembelshem. No matter what you think of me, you know of my mistrust of the King, and I would never put you in harm's way. There has been an amazing transformation in the man. The King, the Special Forces, and those loyal to the Lancaster family have spent the night removing all remnants of those loyal to the Council. The Kingdom of Rembelshem once again is governed by the Lancaster family. Six months ago I would have said that that was a tragedy in itself. At this time of need, the country needs strong leaders for reassurance. At this very moment your uncle knows he holds this country together by a thread. He is the strength for the people, but you hold their hearts. Your uncle needs your help. This country needs your help."

Rebekah looked to the Sisters for reassurance. They both nodded. What was she to do? Did she really have a choice? She was placed in this position for a purpose. To deny it was to deny God. Rebekah swallowed. Just as denying her gifts were to deny God.

"What about Jarod the Great?" Rebekah asked.

"He is fine. He left with the Special Forces this morning carrying a message from the King to halt the army's advance on the Saurian forces. The King is hoping to hear back from Paladin Markos on the subject," Sister Elizabeth said.

Rebekah's heart dropped. She knew it was silly. She had never met the boy. She barely even knew him except through their brief exchange in prison. She hoped someday she would meet and finally see who this Jarod the Great really was. There were so many questions she wanted to ask him.

"I guess we better not keep my uncle waiting. Please lead the way."

* * * *

REBEKAH STARED at the hole in the tower as she followed Phillip and the Sisters toward the castle. And she was supposed to be more powerful than Jarod? That scared her. The memories of the dead Saurian with a hole burned through his chest and the sword of fire she had used to cut off her uncle's arm gave her shivers. She knew it should not, but it did. Jarod had seemed to easily understand and accept what he had been given, why couldn't she? One more reason that she really wanted to meet him.

As Rebekah entered the palace, she thought how wonderful it was to actually look around. Every other time she had ever been in the palace she had tall guards surrounding her. They barely left much room to view the surroundings. It was a wonderful experience to walk through the castle so freely. Phillip led them up to the second floor of the eastern tower toward the throne room. She had never been to the throne room, and she was very anxious to see it. Now that Rebekah thought about it, she really had not seen much of the palace. She had spent most of her time either in her room or, more recently, in the underground cell.

Rebekah laid her hand on her sword hilt. She was not sure what to expect. She would agree with Phillip on one point. She knew he would never lead her into a dangerous situation. He feared the retribution of her father. She had never seen her father perform any act that would be remotely threatening, but she had learned recently there was a lot about her father that she really did not know.

As Phillip approached, the two guards opened the two large wooden doors leading into the throne room. Rebekah's heart was pounding. The first time she had met her uncle ended with him losing an arm. The other times they were enemies within the slave camp. Now she was supposed to be friendly and help him, as if nothing had ever happened? It was one thing to forgive your brother, but it was another to put yourself at risk. She would take it one step at a time and hope Jarod was right about her uncle.

The room was larger than she had expected. It was two stories high and had more gold decorations and white marble than even the entranceway. King Robert sat on a throne at the end of the long room. He was busy arguing with a large group of people. Rebekah walked closer and was surprised to see that the group of people was the refugees from the slave camp. The young Dangarian princess broke away from the group, ran toward Rebekah and gave her a hug. Other members of the group who recognized Rebekah quickly followed, hugging Rebekah and asking how she was doing. Rebekah had forgotten that the last time they had seen her, she had been tortured and then transported away by a dragon.

The room quieted as the King stood up.

"You are the last of the leaders of Dangaria and the Republic. Your countries have been destroyed and your people scattered throughout the lands. Half of Rembelshem has been lost and we cannot defend ourselves much longer against the enemy. There is only one chance we have to survive against this common enemy, and that is to unite as one force and as one nation. Dangaria, the Republic, and Rembelshem will choose four delegates each to represent their lands and to give counsel to the new leader."

"And who shall that leader be? You?" A senator from the Republic shouted.

It was finally making sense to Rebekah. Her uncle had positioned himself to have the ultimate power and take control of the two countries that had been a thorn in his side for so many years. The two countries really had no choice, and he knew it. Without Rembelshem's help, their lands would be lost to the Saurians. This option would allow to them to at least keep some sort of governing position, and it was the best chance to defeat the Saurians.

King Robert raised a hand to stop the growing commotion, and then he smiled. "No. I will be one of the four advisors representing Rembelshem. The leader of our new country will be Queen Rebekah Lancaster."

CHAPTER TWENTY-EIGHT
Preparations for War

"We make war that we may live in peace." - Aristotle (384 BC–322 BC)

"No weapon that is formed against thee shall prosper." - Isaiah 54:17

THE SPECIAL FORCES TEAM stood on the hill overlooking the Rembelshem army encampment. Jarod had been with the army and had an idea of its size, but seeing the whole army from a top-down view was different. Soldiers, tents, and equipment stretched in a straight line in both directions as far as Jarod could see. A mile south, the Saurian army was forming. Though it was not as big as theirs, Jarod knew it was still as deadly. From this distance he could clearly see giant four-legged lizard creatures being herded to form the front line. The giant beasts were covered in armor that glinted in the sun. He was not sure what the human army could do to stop such creatures. Regular arrows and swords would bounce off their thick hide.

A long line of two-legged, dinosaur-like mounts ridden by Saurian riders was forming behind the giant creatures. The creatures were also covered in armor and their riders carried long spears. The human army had a sizeable cavalry, but the horses did not bite the enemy with giant teeth, as the Saurian mounts did. Ostriches. That was what the creatures reminded Jarod of. Giant lizard ostriches. If he had not witnessed so many strange events already, he would not have believed his eyes.

"Move out," Jordan said, leading the men down the hill.

Jarod's shoulder throbbed, but it was tolerable. Thankfully, his chainmail had kept the arrow from piercing too deep. All eight men began walking slowly down the hill toward the back of the encampment. Their uniforms marked their rank, and men quickly moved out of the way. Jordan led the group toward the largest tent.

Several guards lined the outside of the tent and blocked the entrance. Jordan approached the lead guard and said something to him. The guard entered the tent, and then exited, shouting orders to his men. They stepped to the side, allowing the special forces to enter.

Jordan nodded to the lead guard and led his team into the command tent. Jarod had seen the tent during his time with the army, but he had never been inside. The large circular tent was fifty feet across and twenty feet high at the peak. There were men seated at the smaller tables on the outskirts of the tent, but the central focus was a large wooden table with maps and papers littered across it set close to the middle of the tent. Several men stood around the table discussing suggestions and plans for the upcoming battle.

Those gathered in the tent grew silent as the eight special forces entered. The big black man who towered over the rest of them was obviously the General. His solid gaze fell on each of the men. Jarod noticed the six foot broadsword on the giant man's back, and he knew the man could attack with it before any of them could make it half way toward the table.

Jarod also recognized Captain Darian. The captain of ancient Asian descent also noticed Jarod, and he smiled as he stepped forward. His bald head was covered with a fur-lined cap and his brown eyes sparkled.

"Jarod, it is so good to see you. The uniform looks good on you," Captain Darian said, clasping Jarod's arm as he shook it.

"It is good to see you safe and well, Captain Darian."

"What brings the Special Forces team here? I hope you are not here to teach any lessons."

Jarod smiled at the remark. "No. Commander Jordan will explain."

Jordan approached the General and handed the big man a rolled parchment. The General looked at the wax seal.

"This is King Robert's mark?"

"King Robert once again controls Rembelshem."

The General laid a hand on the hilt that stuck over his head and eyed Jordan and the rest of the Special Forces team.

"No, no. We are not here for that. So much has happened I forgot you were wanted by the King at one time. As far as the King is concerned, you still lead the army as appointed by the Princess."

"What of the Council and the Princess?"

"The Princess is safe with the Sisters and the Council," Jordan paused and looked at Jarod, "will no longer be a problem."

The General glanced at Jordan, and then at Jarod. He then broke the seal on the scroll. He read the scroll, looked at Jordan with a strange look, and then re-read the scroll.

"Is this some type of joke? Dragons?"

"As much of a joke as intelligent lizard creatures preparing for a battle a mile away," Jordan replied.

"Point taken. We hold our position until further notice," the General said, passing the scroll to Captain Darian. The General turned back to Jordan. "Now that you are here, your team can help with a problem we have. We have received reports of mysterious deaths throughout our ranks in the army. A soldier will be standing, and then lying on the ground dead, as if an invisible weapon had struck him. You are not surprised. Who is doing this?"

Jordan looked at his team then back at the General. "They are called the Psi'Drakor. They are the special forces of the Saurians who are invisible," Jordan said, motioning a hand toward his men. "Jarod, you getting anything?"

Jarod closed his eyes. Since there were so many Saurians in the area, he had been ignoring the dots in his mind. There was the long line parallel to the human army, but there were also many scouts roaming in the vicinity. Jarod walked to the table and looked at the primary map of the area. The General and leaders had small figures marking the locations of the armies and war equipment. Jarod tried to overlay the dots in his head onto the map. He could visualize the other dots that were not part of the main army roaming the landscape. The Special Forces team encircled the table. Jarod placed a finger on the map between the armies.

"A group of ten Psi'Drakor approach here." Jarod moved his finger to a new location on the map. "Another group is quickly heading toward our current location. I advise we move all from this tent."

"Agreed. Michael can four of you handle them?"

"Gladly. They will be quite surprised at the trap that has been set."

"Good. Jarod. You monitor the situation from outside. We will handle each Saurian Psi'Drakor squad one at a time. General and Captain, please allow us to escort you to a safe distance."

Jarod gathered the four men into a huddle.

"Stay alert, be strong, and keep the faith. Let us pray."

Jordan, Sven, and Gilbert hurriedly escorted

the group of soldiers out of the tent. The General stayed behind and watched the five Special Forces members pray.

Once the prayer ended, Jarod headed toward the tent exit. He paused when he noticed the tears in the General's eyes.

"Everything alright, sir?"

"Yes, yes. My Grandma would have been pleased to see this day. The King's men praying. I think I would have believed in dragons before I would have believed that. I have to hear this story," the General said. He put his arm around Jarod and both exited from the tent.

* * * *

THE PSI'DRAKOR WERE closing in on the tent. The guards and most of the soldiers had been removed from the tent area to prevent as much human death as possible.

Jarod swallowed nervously as he watched the events unfold. Was the team ready to do this on their own? He was starting to understand what parents feel as they release a child into the world. Had they trained them and prepared them enough for the world? Jarod felt the same. He had tried to teach the others all that he had learned in such a short amount of time. He knew they could not live by his faith, but they must learn and grow on their own.

"The Saurians are about to enter the tent," Jarod whispered to the others as they hid behind wagons and tents.

The ten Psi'Drakor rushed the tent and the sound of metal against metal rang throughout the area. Within a minute the sounds of battle stopped. The tension was high, but Jarod let out a sigh of relief. Even before the Special Forces team exited the tent, he knew they had succeeded. The Saurian dots in his mind had disappeared.

CHAPTER TWENTY-NINE
Dragon Army

"I know war as few other men now living know it, and nothing to me is more revolting. I have long advocated its complete abolition, as its very destructiveness on both friend and foe has rendered it useless as a method of settling international disputes."
- General Douglas Macarthur (1880 - 1964)

MARKOS'S EYES CLOSED, and he jumped when he felt his head nodding. Markos shook his head to wake up. Sjvek had been flying throughout the night, and the warm air they were now encountering was making it hard for Markos to stay awake.

We are almost there. The southwest dragon lair entrance is in the large canyon ahead.

It is too dark. I cannot see the ground. Are you talking about the Grand Canyon?

Yes, that is how the humans refer to it.

Markos peered over the side of the dragon, but he could not see anything.

I have always wanted to see the Grand Canyon. How long are we staying?

We will leave in the morning. I will need a slight rest to make the flight back.

Markos felt encouraged. He would be able to see the Grand Canyon from the air. He could not ask for a better way to see it.

Markos could feel Sjvek's body start to slow and descend. Markos looked but still could not see the ground.

How do you know where to land?

Dragons have night vision. I do not see anything in color. It is all in a grayscale tone, but I can still see everything rather well.

That knowledge made Markos feel more comfortable. This was the first time they had flown together at night, and the thought of flying into the side of a mountain did not appeal to Markos.

Markos briefly saw the top of the canyon wall as Sjvek tilted his body and descended past ground level. Markos held onto the saddle as Sjvek turned in a new direction, and then maneuvered his body into a landing. Markos didn't see the cave entrance until they were ten feet away from it. The mouth of the cave was large enough for Sjvek to easily flap his wings into a soft landing inside.

Markos slid off the back of Sjvek and took off the saddle.

"So what do we do now?"

You will stay here and I will return for you.

I do not get to see where the dragons live?

It is not advisable. I do not know how the others will handle the news. I also cannot guarantee your safety.

There is no telling what the dragonlings might do to you. They are quite wild in their young age, and they do not always think logically.

I understand. Many humans are illogical even after they grow up. How big are the dragonlings?

A newborn dragon hatchling is the size of a human. The older version, the dragonling, is slightly more independent and is allowed to roam. They are the size of one of your smaller horses. Once the dragonlings grow slightly larger than a big horse, like the one you have always ridden, they will learn how to fly. So you would be walking around a dark cave with various sizes of dragonlings running around. As I have stated, it is in your best interest to stay here.

Markos shuddered as he envisioned multiple dragonlings the size of Duke chasing after him in a dark cave.

No problem.

I also suggest that you stay to the side of the cave. There is no telling who may be landing or leaving. I will be back by morning.

Markos watched as the dragon walked deeper into the cave. Markos had never thought about how a dragon would walk, but as he watched Sjvek it occurred to him that they walked like other reptiles he had seen. They had the same odd twist of the body as a salamander when they walked.

Odd?

Markos blushed. *Well, um, it just was not what I was expecting. Sorry. Was that humor that I sensed?*

Maybe.

* * * *

MARKOS SAT on the edge of the cave and watched the sun rise. The cave was a few hundred feet above the canyon floor, which allowed Markos to see for a considerable distance across the canyon.

He had been awake for a couple hours, since he had not been able to sleep very well. He had never tried to sleep anywhere worse than on the rocky cave floor, but the thought of being trampled by an arriving dragon or being dragged away by a wild dragonling kept him awake.

Markos could sense a dragon coming from deep within the cave behind him. He was thankful for that ability. If a dragon were to surprise him while he was sitting on the edge of the canyon wall, he would have a very long fall.

Markos stood up and moved over next to the cave wall. He could not tell if the dragon was Sjvek, so it was better to be out of the way.

It is I.

Thank you for the clarification. How did it go?

Well. The news has already spread across the different dragon locations. Those in support of my mother have already moved to the central location. Most will support our cause, and few will stay because they are undecided. They will be coming soon, so apply the saddle so we can leave. We have four more locations to visit.

Markos quickly strapped the saddle onto Sjvek, and then climbed on and strapped himself in.

They will be here soon.

How many will there be?

Twenty-six.

Markos felt slightly anxious. He would be nervous meeting twenty-six humans, let alone twenty-six dragons. After a minute passed, Markos could sense the dragons coming from deep within the cave.

Sjvek stepped off the edge of the cave and let his body freefall toward the canyon floor. After a couple seconds he began to flap his wings to slow their descent. He flapped his wings harder and they began to climb above the canyon walls. Markos looked at the huge canyon in the morning sun. It was more magnificent than he could ever have imagined. Markos turned and looked back. The group of dragons was launching into the sky from the cave mouth. Markos was not sure which was more magnificent: the canyon or watching twenty-six assorted color dragons flying behind him and Sjvek.

That is only twenty-six. Wait until we have hundreds.

Markos could not wait. He relaxed and enjoyed the scenery as they flew east.

CHAPTER THIRTY
Attack!

"You may deceive all the people part of the time, and part of the people all the time, but not all the people all the time." - Abraham Lincoln

Y*OU HAVE done well. The human army will be destroyed quickly.*

The Saurian Queen had not expected the Voice. It had been almost two weeks since her last communication with the Voice.

Yes. Their army is double our size, but that is not big enough.

The humans will lose a quarter of their army during the beginning of the battle. Their species is notorious for weak-minded combatants that flee during such battles.

Hopefully they do not. The more we destroy today the less we need to cleanse from the world later.

You must begin your attack now.

We are not fully prepared. We still have two more days before the full force arrives.

It does not matter. Prepare your troops now. Time is crucial.

We have plenty of time. Why rush?

Do not argue with me, Saurian. Do as I say or die. Now go.

The Queen looked over the troops from near her tent atop the hill. Never had so many Saurians been in one location. She looked further north and could see the disgusting human army a mile away. She might not like the Voice, but their goals were the same: to rid the planet of the vile human species.

"Prepare the troops. The final battle begins now," the Queen said to the General standing by her side.

CHAPTER THIRTY-ONE
To Stop a War

"Never, never, never believe any war will be smooth and easy, or that any-one who embarks on the strange voyage can measure the tides and hurri-canes he will encounter. The statesman who yields to war fever must realize that once the signal is given, he is no longer the master of policy but the slave of unforeseeable and uncontrollable events."

- Sir Winston Churchill (1874–1965)

A SOLDIER PULLED his looking glass away from his eye and looked at the General. "The Saurians are preparing to move, sir."

The General took the looking glass from the soldier and used it to look across the open field at the Saurian army.

"That does not make sense. Our scouts reported that their army is still forming. Why would they attack now?"

Jarod looked at the Saurian army with his own looking glass. The other Special Forces were doing the same as they all stood on guard around the General and the captains. Indeed, they were preparing to charge. Some Saurians were climbing onto the elephant-sized lizard mounts, while others were saddling and mounting the two-legged lizard creatures.

The General shouted orders. His broad smile and sense of humor were nowhere to be found. This was the General under whom the Outlaw City had reformed. Even the Special Forces members backed away from the big man.

Jarod continued watching as the giant lizard creature's mounts began to move. Each leg could easily step on and squash any human soldier. He highly doubted if regular arrows would even be able to penetrate their armor and hide. The army had begun creating six foot crossbows to defend against the beasts, but they were not yet ready.

With his gifts, Jarod thought he might be able to take care of one. But that was only one. There were hundreds of creatures lined up and walking toward the human army. Though he wanted to do more, he could not leave his position. The Special Forces had been instructed to protect the leaders in case the Psi'Drakor tried a sneak attack during the chaos of the battle.

But the approaching army was not what was bothering Jarod. There was something else coming, but he did not know what it was. He sensed two separate large groups heading toward them from the west. Jarod turned the looking glass to the west to find the two new groups he was sensing. He let out a moan, which caused the others to look to the west as well.

He had no clue what the new creatures were, but there was an army of them. Even from this distance he could tell that the lizard creatures were much larger than the regular Saurians. Jarod had to do a double take when he passed at the front of the army. Yes, it was what he thought he saw; a human and a normal Saurian were leading the creatures.

"It is Prince Daniel," the soldiers began to whisper.

The Prince and the Saurian led the other creatures directly between the middle of the Saurian and human armies. Jarod looked at the Prince. There was something very familiar about him. Maybe he had seen him in the Royal Palace.

Jarod looked for the other force that was approaching. He searched everywhere to the west, but he could see nothing. Then thundering roars shook the ground as hundreds of dragons materialized in the sky and flew close to the ground between the armies. They landed on the eastern space between the armies, beside Prince Daniel and his giant creatures to the west.

Some members of the Saurian army hesitated, while others advanced. The dragons roared more violently as the two armies were separated now by only a half mile. A single pink dragon ridden by a man swooped from the sky, breathing a blast of fire into the grassy plain and causing the rest of the Saurian army to stop.

Jarod knew that the rider was Paladin Markos, and he watched as the dragon landed gracefully alongside the other dragons. Markos slid from the dragon's back and walked boldly as over a hundred dragons loomed above him. Markos walked past the dragons toward the advancing Prince Daniel.

Shock and awe ran throughout the human army as they witnessed a sight that they never could have dreamed of seeing. Jarod and the Special Forces had seen the dragons, and they knew they existed. But the rest of the men were now dealing with the reality of the situation. A year ago life was simple. The men in the army were preparing to defend their country against an invasion that may come from a neighboring country. Now they were standing defensively against an invading intelligent lizard species, and they had just witnessed the myth of dragons. A year ago, Jarod was attending school and hiding from the school bully most of the time. That school bully now stood next to him as a brother in arms and a brother in faith.

Paladin Markos bowed to the Saurian and locked arms to greet with Prince Daniel. Two of the large Saurian creatures followed the Saurian toward their army and Paladin Markos. Prince Daniel turned and walked toward the human army.

"Paladin Markos and Prince Daniel working with a Saurian and dragons. This is going to be an interesting story. Jordan, bring your men," the General said as he walked past the Special Forces barrier and down the hill.

"Jarod and Billy, guard the captains. The rest of you come with me," Jordan ordered.

CHAPTER THIRTY-TWO
Compromised

"The ultimate measure of a man is not where he stands in moments of comfort and convenience, but where he stands at times of challenge and controversy." - Martin Luther King Jr. (1929 - 1968)

"When one door closes another door opens; but we so often look so long and so regretfully upon the closed door, that we do not see the ones which open for us." - Alexander Graham Bell (1847 - 1922)

I ZIKAR ENTERED and eyed the six guards standing around the large tent. He bowed to the Queen as she sat on her throne.

"Your Majesty, it is an honor to be in your presence again," Izikar said.

"Arc'Reisheen, your presence is a surprise. We believed you were captured or dead. I am, however, disappointed with your means of returning. You have disobeyed my edict regarding the trolls, and you have purposely disrupted our annihilation of the humans."

"All can be explained, and there is a purpose. Your Majesty, please listen carefully. I know you have been in communicating with and receiving instructions from a third party. But you have been tricked."

"What have the humans done to you, that you dare question my authority and bring such allegations?"

"The third party deceiving you is the Queen of the Dragons."

"Arc,Reisheen, you above all people know that the dragons have no intelligence. Your Psi'Drakor observed numerous times and learned their secrets. They would have found out otherwise."

"I assure you, Your Majesty, I have met a dragon and they have abilities, even beyond our own, to comprehend complex equations and matters. Their queen has planned this war for many years. She does not want the trolls to be on the surface, lest she be forced to face a great opponent. Once the Saurian and human battle is finished, the dragons plan to kill both the human and Saurian survivors."

"Even if your allegations were true, we have the trolls now. The dragons have not harmed us. We can finish this battle and cleanse the land of the humans. Then we will deal with the dragons with the help of the trolls. I do not see any problems."

Izikar shook his head. He had been around the human too long. Even his own people were sounding arrogant to him.

"The dragons have sided with those meaning us harm. I ask that you halt the army until we can clearly determine what is happening."

"You are not thinking logically Arc'Reisheen. I can only assume that the humans have done something to you. You will be placed under arrest until you can be examined," the Queen said. She nodded to her guards.

Izikar sighed. After centuries of his lineage being Arc'Reisheen, he would have to be the one to use the Arc'Reisheen Decree.

"I am sorry, Your Majesty. It is you who will be placed under arrest. Your leadership has been compromised, and I cannot be certain that you are thinking for yourself. I hereby implement the Arc'Reisheen Decree and remove you from power until further notice."

As Izikar finished the announcement, four Psi'Drakor materialized in the tent and aimed their weapons at the Queen's guards.

"We may war against the humans someday, but it will be on our own terms…not the dragons'," Izikar said to the Queen.

CHAPTER THIRTY-THREE
The Enemy

"*How wonderful it is that nobody need wait a single moment before starting to improve the world.*" - Anne Frank (1929 - 1945), Diary of a Young Girl, 1952

MARKOS TURNED his head and looked at the large creatures. "So those are Trolls, huh?"

"Unbelievable, is it not? They do not look like it, but they are more similar to humans than the smaller Saurian race. I have to show you this game they play. It is rather fun."

"You played games with a troll?"

Daniel shrugged his shoulders. "They are as much a victim of the Saurians as we are. Their power in the underground dwellings is sporadic. Once it is totally destroyed, they will be locked down there with no lights and no way to get out."

Daniel looked at the human army and rubbed his wrist. It was not home, but it was closer than he had been in a while. Daniel could see soldiers move to the side as the General, escorted by a team of Special Forces, walked toward them. He recognized Jordan. This was his chance to finally get his hands on Jarod and show everybody that he was an imposter. That boy had put too many lives at risk, and it had to end. Daniel scanned the other Special Forces but they were all too old, and they were obviously not Jarod.

"Prince Daniel. Paladin Markos. It is so good to see you. Your timing could not have been better. I tried to hold as ordered, but the Saurians left us no choice," the General said with a bow.

"General, it is a pleasure as always. You were ordered to hold?" Markos looked at Jordan. "I assume your mission to free the Princess was successful?"

"Ah…not exactly as planned. Nevertheless, the Princess has been freed and she was safe with the Sisters when we left. King Robert once again controls Rembelshem, and he gave the orders based on your information," Jordan replied.

"You left Rebekah alone with Robert as King? What happened to the Council?" Daniel asked.

"I assure you. The Princess does not need to worry about the King, Your Highness. He has changed and he is not the man he once was. The Council? Well, that is harder to explain. You will understand when you return to Lansing. Let me just say that Jarod the Great dealt with them, and they will no longer be a problem."

"Jarod the Great," Daniel spat. "Where is he?! I do not know what tricks he has played, but this will end now!"

Jordan looked confused. "Tricks? I am not sure what you are referring to. Jarod is standing guard to protect the others at the war room tent."

"Bring him here. Send another who can actually do the job the boy is pretending to do."

"I…yes, Your Highness. Michael please replace Jarod."

"Yes, sir," Michael said as he hurriedly ran back up the hill toward the large tent.

* * * *

JAROD WATCHED as Michael quickly approached.

"Jarod, Prince Daniel is requesting that you join them."

"Me? Why?"

Michael shrugged. "He acted like he knows you. Have you met the Prince before?"

Jarod shook his head. "Never."

"I do not know, then. I would hurry, though. He seems to be in a foul mood."

Jarod rushed past the soldiers as he headed toward the Prince and the others. He was finally going to meet Prince Daniel and Paladin Markos. The Prince had picked him to join the Special Forces, and Jarod was anxious to meet the man who had given him the opportunity. Jarod wondered about the Prince's anger. Maybe the Prince was upset about what Jarod had done to the Royal Palace. Or maybe he was personally requesting Jarod for another mission. He could not wait to find out.

As he reached the outskirts of the army he could see the small group gathered in the open grass field. The whole group turned and looked his way as he broke past the edge of the human army. He saw the Prince staring at him intensely. Jarod recognized something about those eyes…something vaguely familiar. Jarod's thoughts suddenly changed as the power began surging through him and the colorful land abruptly turned into the black and white particles. Jarod could see six invisible Psi'Drakor surrounding three Saurians and two of the large Saurian creatures. They were crossing the grassy field and headed toward the Prince and others. Jarod pulled his two swords from his back scabbard and ran toward the group of humans.

* * * *

DANIEL WATCHED as the boy in the Special Forces uniform ran towards them. The boy's hair was cut short, and he was nowhere near as scrawny as he was when Daniel had last seen him. If Daniel hadn't traveled with the boy, he would not have recognized him as the whiney, lazy kid from his home town. Although the boy had grown up rapidly and now looked the part of a Special Forces Officer, Daniel knew Jarod had minimal weapon skills. How the boy had fooled Jordan was still a mystery, but one that would be solved very soon.

Daniel had seen many strange things in the last few months, but nothing like seeing the boy's eyes suddenly turn into streaming light radiating from the sockets. Jarod grabbed the two swords from his back and ran faster toward them. Daniel stepped back and pulled out his sword to defend himself. The other Special Forces' eyes suddenly changed and looked like

Jarod's. What madness was this?

"Daniel, it is alright," Markos said as he gently pushed Daniel's sword point to the ground with his axe. "Look," Markos said as he motioned to Izikar and two other Saurians returning with the two trolls.

The other Special Forces members' eyes began to glow just like Jarod's. They all drew their weapons and Jarod joined the group as they circled the human commanders.

"Let them pass, Jordan," Daniel said.

* * * *

THE SPECIAL FORCES stopped circling and allowed the three Saurians and two trolls to pass. The six Psi'Drakor stayed on the outside and circled as they studied the Special Forces team.

One of them passed by Jarod. The creature knew it could be seen, and it was not as invincible as it once thought. Jarod had never been so close to one in this state without killing it. He knew the others wanted to attack the same as he did. He was sure these Psi'Drakor knew they were the ones that had killed their fellow Psi'Drakors, and wanted to attack them as well.

"What trickery is this, human?"

"I do not know. Markos?" Prince Daniel asked.

"The dragons gave you an advantage over the humans by teaching your Psi'Drakor to be invisible, but God has provided us with a means to achieve a balance."

"A god?" Izikar spat. "You humans are so illogical."

"You only recently learned that the dragons are a smarter species than yourselves, and they live on Earth. Do you really think you can comprehend the equations of one that lives in the Universe? There is far more to this world than you can imagine, let alone what is beyond it," Paladin Markos replied.

"An investigation is underway into the accusations that the dragons have instigated this war. You will draw your forces back and we will have a cease fire agreement until we can determine what harm has been done," Izikar said.

"And if your investigation is inconclusive?" Prince Daniel asked.

"Then you and I may still have our battle against each other," Izikar said.

CHAPTER THIRTY-FOUR
Reunited

"Duty is ours, results are God's."
- John Quincy Adams (1767 - 1848)

"I will sing of the mercies of the LORD for ever: with my mouth will I make known thy faithfulness to all generations." - Psalms 89:1

D ANIEL GAPED at the hole in the palace tower. "Jarod did that?"

"From what I have been told, yes," Markos replied, looking just as awestruck at the damage.

"Now I am rather glad I never fought him," Daniel said.

"I agree. Between him and what Rebekah can do, the plan is far more than I can comprehend," Markos said.

Daniel grabbed Markos's sleeve and stopped him.

"What do you mean by *what Rebekah can do*?"

Markos looked at Daniel quizzically. "You do not know?" Markos paused to think. "Of course you do not. I have seen Rebekah do things similar to that," Markos said as he pointed toward the gaping hole in the tower. "She may be more powerful than Jarod. He has accepted his position and gifts, but she has yet to do that."

Daniel swallowed. "But she is just my little girl."

"In the physical world, your little girl is the most powerful human on this continent. She now rules over all three countries. That has not happened since before the storms began. If God wishes for her to be the most powerful human in the spiritual world as well, who are we to say?" Markos answered.

Daniel released Markos's sleeve and began walking toward the palace.

"I have not seen Rebekah as a Princess or witnessed what you have seen her do. The last day I saw her she had gone to school, and then she was helping me in my inn. That is the Rebekah I know. We lived a simple, but happy life."

"It shall be interesting to see the Queen, then," Markos said with a smile.

Several guards blocked the entrance into the palace, but Daniel was quickly allowed past and directed to the Queen. Daniel's heart raced. Rebekah was actually in the palace. There was no battle going on or kidnapping that would deter him from finding her again. Daniel forced himself not to race up the stairs to the second level. Daniel and Markos reached the landing of the second level. The throne room doors stood just down the hallway. Daniel paused and pressed out his tunic. It was the same outfit he had worn on the battlefield. Sjvek had carried Markos and Daniel directly from the battlefield to the outskirts of Lansing. That was an adventure that Daniel was sure he would not want to experience again. He had been deeper within Earth and flown higher above the Earth than any human since the days of the Ancients. As with his daughter, his own life was not so simple anymore.

"Ready?" Markos asked.

Daniel nodded and walked toward the door. The guards recognized Daniel, and they bowed and opened the two large wooden doors. The throne room had not changed much in the last sixteen years since he had been gone. But the minor changes in the throne room were far from his mind. He was startled when he saw Rebekah sitting on the throne talking with a small group of people.

She was definitely not his little girl anymore. She looked much older and wiser than when he had last seen her. She was dressed in an intricate white dress embroidered with gold. She wore ornate gold jewelry on her head and around her neck. Daniel smiled. Rebekah was defiantly rebuking the crowd, and she was not backing down.

His brother stood beside her, quietly watching and observing. It had been sixteen years since he had seen his brother – when Daniel had fled from the palace in fear of his brother. His brother was rumored to have been involved in the mysterious death of his wife, and Daniel had feared for the safety of his newborn daughter. Daniel had lived a long time with a hidden identity in fear that the King's men might find him and his daughter. Now his brother stood beside her almost as a body guard, watching the moves of the people around her. He stood as an imposing figure, even with his right arm partially missing. Daniel didn't know that his brother had been in an accident.

Robert looked up and saw his brother for the first time in many years. The two brothers locked eyes for a moment, studying each other. Robert nodded to Daniel in acknowledgement, and then leaned forward and whispered into Rebekah's ear. Rebekah looked up from her conversation with the older gentlemen, and the seriousness on her face melted away as she recognized her father and her uncle.

The queen Daniel had just seen seemed to

vanish as the young girl he knew appeared. Rebekah rushed down the steps leading from the throne and past the group of people. She jumped into Daniel's arms and clung to his neck tightly without letting go. Daniel could not help but cry. He could finally hold the daughter whom he had searched for so long. Rebekah cried as well. After a minute she let go of his neck, and he set her on the ground before him. Daniel wiped the tears from his eyes and tried to compose himself.

"I didn't know if I would ever see you again. What happened to you?" Rebekah asked.

"A very long story. One that is almost unbelievable. We have returned from the battlefield. A ceasefire has been enacted until the information about the dragons is researched further."

Robert escorted the people from the throne room and closed the wooden doors as they left. He returned to Daniel, Markos, and Rebekah.

Daniel held out his right hand, but then swapped it for his left hand to shake his brother's left hand. Robert walked past the hand and embraced Daniel. Daniel was caught off guard. He could not remember ever having hugged his brother. Robert pulled back.

"My brother, it is so good to finally see you again," Robert said.

"Robert," Daniel said, "I will not lie. This is a surreal meeting. Never did I expect that the three of us would be in the same room together. For all her life I have feared such a meeting. I am glad it has finally happened in this manner rather than the other," Daniel said.

"Agreed," Robert said. Then he turned to Markos, "Paladin Markos," he finished with a nod.

Markos nodded in acknowledgement.

Daniel looked down at Rebekah and smiled. It didn't matter what position she now held or what she had done, she was, and would always be, his little girl.

"How did you get back from the battlefield so fast? Oh, you rode Sjvek! What did you think of that?" Rebekah asked excitedly.

"That is something I would rather not do again."

Markos chuckled. "Well, another one to add to my list of those who will not be a Dragon Rider."

CHAPTER THIRTY-FIVE
Understanding Death

*"Thy sun shall no more go down; neither shall thy moon withdraw itself:
for the LORD shall be thine everlasting light, and the days of thy mourn-
ing shall be ended."* - Isaiah 60:20

JAROD DROPPED to his knees and was forced to lean on the tombstone. He thought he could handle the sight of Thadius's grave, but too many memories of the young boy were flooding down on him. Jarod couldn't stop crying. Thadius's curly blonde hair and cheerful smile filled Jarod's mind. Jarod felt a hand being laid on his shoulder.

"Jarod?" asked a female voice.

Jarod took a deep breath, refocused his thoughts, and then stood up.

"I am alright, Sister Elizabeth. Thank you. Thank you for bringing me here. I have seen death and I have dealt death, but this is the hardest thing I have had to do."

"You spoke with Paladin Markos and understand all Thadius was able to do?"

"Yes. Separating the physical world from the spiritual world is still hard to do, though. I was not aware that Thad played such a vital role in helping the Queen call upon her gifts – similar to the role he played in helping me find out who I am. His life was not in vain, but his death is still hard to deal with."

"Take as much time as you need. I will be in

that building there," Sister Elizabeth said, pointing toward a stone building.

Jarod nodded and then turned back to Thadius's tombstone.

CHAPTER THIRTY-SIX
Awards Ceremony

"Faith is the substance of things hoped for, the evidence of things not seen."
- Hebrews 11:1

"But without faith it is impossible to please him: for he that cometh to God must believe that he is, and that he is a rewarder of them that diligently seek him." - Hebrews 11:6

JAROD BUTTONED the last button on his Special Forces dress uniform. He looked into the mirror and adjusted the tight collar. He had never worn such a formal and decorative outfit in his life.

"It looks good," Jordan said, slapping Jarod on the back. "It is not every day a soldier gets the honor of receiving a medal from a Queen."

"I know. I am just nervous. Give me a squad of Saurians any day. I hate being the center of attention. At least it is not just me. The rest of you will also be receiving medals," Jarod explained.

Jordan laughed. "You better stop your great achievements if you do not want to be noticed."

Jarod could not help but laugh. It felt good to laugh. He did not think he had laughed since his last few days with Thadius.

The eight Special Forces members finished dressing in their navy blue, high-necked dress tunics in the large dressing room. It was an odd sight for Jarod. He was used to seeing these same men in their Special Forces black armor, covered in dirt or blood with scowls on their faces. Each of them now had showered, dressed in the intricate blue and gold outfits, and were smiling. Once upon a time he would not have dared turn his back on any of them. Now, he would trust his life with any of them.

"It's time," a servant announced.

Jarod's heart began to pound. He had seen all the people flowing into the throne room. He would also finally get to meet the Princess. Jarod shook his head. He meant the Queen. That would be an embarrassing mistake. It would be nice to see King Robert. Jarod thought again. It would be nice to see Prince Robert again. This royalty business was strange and confusing stuff.

Jordan lined the eight men in a row and positioned Jarod last. "For freeing the Queen, and for your long list of achievements, it has been requested that you be last."

"You could not have warned me a little earlier?" Jarod asked. He knew what this meant. He could not easily slide between the others receiving their medals. The attention would be on him for the climax of the ceremony.

Jordan smiled. "And let you have all that time to fret about it. No."

Jordan took his position at the front of the line and led the men out of the room. They climbed the stairs to the second level and waited outside the wooden doors leading into the throne room. The Special Forces team adjusted and patted their uniforms one more time, and then Jordan nodded to the guards who were holding the door handles.

The two guards opened the doors and a wave of murmurs rolled across the room. Jarod leaned to the side, looking past Michael's big shoulders. There had to be over a thousand finely dressed people in the room. Jarod swallowed nervously. He hoped this would go quick.

* * * *

REBEKAH FORCED HERSELF not to tap her foot. She had never been around so many people in one room before. Her father and her uncle stood on each side of her throne, which was reassuring. She was dressed in the most elaborate dress and jewelry she had ever worn. She hated the thought that others might think she was arrogant and snobbish, or that others thought she was better than everybody else because she was the Queen. She was far from being that person.

Her father bent down slightly and said, "You are doing well. It should not last that long. It must be strange for you as the Queen to give medals to Billy and Jarod."

"Billy Thompson. Yes, I know. He has come a long way. Circumstances have never allowed me to meet Jarod the Great. It will be nice to finally meet him."

"You do not know who Jarod the Great is?" Daniel asked. The doors to the throne room opened. The crowd turned toward the Special Forces members as they came walking through the doorway. "Oh, this should be interesting," he added with a smile as he straightened up into his position.

Rebekah was confused, but she could not ask him what he meant. The blonde-haired Jordan led his team toward her, and she was handed the first medal.

* * * *

JAROD KEPT HIS HEAD down. As long as he could not see the people staring at him, they were not really staring at him, right? He knew it wasn't true, but it was comforting to him.

A hush came over the crowd as the Queen began to announce Jordan's achievements. The room burst into applause as Jordan was given his medal. One by one the Queen announced the Special Forces members' names. The only good thing, Jarod thought, was that he would finally get to meet the Queen who was as gifted as he was. Jarod's heart was racing. It was his turn.

"And finally, one who's name even the Saurians know, Jarod the Great!" the Queen shouted.

The crowd erupted into deafening applause. Jarod could feel his face turning red as he stared down at the floor tiles.

"Jarod the Great, for your courage on the battlefield during the siege, your help with freeing the rulers of all three lands, and for freeing me from the dungeons below, I award you with the Rembelshem Medal of Honor!" More applause followed.

Jarod kept his head down as the Queen placed

the medal around his neck. It was finally over.

Jarod lifted his head to thank the Queen, but he lost the words as he stared at the Queen. He knew only one person in his life with such blue eyes.

"Rebekah Smith?" Jarod asked in utter confusion.

* * * *

REBEKAH STUDIED Jarod the Great. He looked vaguely familiar. Nobody knew her as Rebekah Smith. How did he? Only the people from Kalkaska knew her by that name; and Billy Thompson had already received his medal. Her father knew. He had mentioned it. Rebekah glanced left toward her father for answers. From the smirk on his face, she could tell he was enjoying her moment of confusion. He bent down and whispered in her ear.

Rebekah looked back toward Jarod in disbelief.

"Jarod O'Grady?"

Queen Rebekah Ann Lancaster

Artwork in *Into the Darkness* was rendered using:

DAZ Productions' DazStudio

www.daz3d.com

Characters and clothing created using DAZ products.

Faith of the Unforgotten
Book One of The Foundations of Hope Trilogy
Into the Darkness
Book Two of The Foundations of Hope Trilogy
Dawn of a New Hope
Book Three of The Foundations of Hope Trilogy

Sign up for The Foundations of Hope mailing list at:
www.foundationsofhope.com